Voices Of The Future

Edited by Emily Wilson

First published in Great Britain in 2016 by:

Remus House
Coltsfoot Drive
Peterborough
PE2 9BF
Telephone: 01733 890066
Website: www.youngwriters.co.uk

Book Design by Ashley Janson

SB ISBN 978-1-78624-247-1

Printed and bound in the UK by BookPrintingUK
Website: www.bookprintinguk.com

Foreword

Welcome, Reader!

For Young Writers' latest competition, *Poetry Emotions*, we gave school children nationwide the task of writing a poem all about emotions, and they rose to the challenge magnificently!

Pupils could either write about emotions they've felt themselves or create a character to represent an emotion. Which one they chose was entirely up them. Our aspiring poets have also developed their creative skills along the way, getting to grips with poetic techniques such as rhyme, simile and alliteration to bring their thoughts to life. The result is this entertaining collection that allows us a fascinating glimpse into the minds of the next generation, giving us an insight into their innermost feelings. It also makes a great keepsake for years to come.

Here at Young Writers our aim is to encourage creativity in children and to inspire a love of the written word, so it's great to get such an amazing response, with some absolutely fantastic poems. This made it a tough challenge to pick the winners, so well done to *Brooke Evans-Harries* who has been chosen as the best author in this anthology.

I'd like to congratulate all the young authors in *Poetry Emotions – Voices Of The Future* – I hope this inspires them to continue with their creative writing.

Jenni Bannister

Editorial Manager

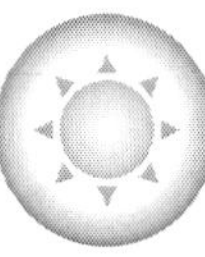

Our charity partner for this academic year is . . .

YOUNGMINDS

The voice for young people's **mental health and wellbeing**

We're aiming to raise a huge £5,000 this academic year to help raise awareness for YoungMinds and the great work they do to support children and young people.

If you would like to get involved visit
www.justgiving.com/Young-Writers

YoungMinds is the UK's leading charity committed to improving the emotional wellbeing and mental health of children and young people. They campaign, research and influence policy and practice on behalf of children and young people to improve care and services. They also provide expert knowledge to professionals, parents and young people through the Parents' Helpline, online resources, training and development, outreach work and publications. Their mission is to improve the emotional resilience of all children and to ensure that those who suffer ill mental health get fast and effective support.

www.youngminds.org.uk

Contents

Sampford Peverell Primary School, Tiverton

Stoke Bishop CE Primary School, Bristol

Stottesdon CE Primary School, Kidderminster

The Poems

Emotions

It's no surprise
That it creeps up my spine
It chews me up and then spits me out
I plead with Fear to stop toying with my emotions.

It's better than paradise
And better that bed
It's as gold as Rushy Bay's sand
Joy, don't leave me!

Deep blue
Maybe mournful
It's said that crying helps let it all out
But Sadness lets no comfort in.

Throwing your things around
Red, red, red
Deciding to fight back
Red vehemence is the least Anger could give you.

The worst of Anger and Sadness
Is something you panic about
Day and night
Anxiety haunts you.

Hide behind a curtain of hair
Or behind your mum
Silent as a tree
Shy helps you learn the importance of silence
And prevents you from knowing people well.

Nidhi Joshi (10)

Hate

Hate is red like a sea of blood,
He tastes like the sour and salty sea,
He smells like a burning fire,
He looks like a burning hot, red potato,
He sounds like the croaking of frogs
And he feels like a burnt marshmallow.

Jack Turner (9)

Friendless

Away from family,
While others skip happily.
Away from friends,
Only other people stay,
To take them away,
So there's people to play.
Just sorrow left,
To spend the day.
Not even a pay,
Will find another way,
To say,
I'm not alone

The only thing you'll know
Is that you can't go,
You are friendless.

Louisa Angelina Gregory (9)
All Saints CE (VA) Primary School , Wellingborough

Happiness Is Kind

H appiness is nice
A time of love
P laying in the hot, beaming sun
P amper night with my friends
I love my family, it is like a dream come true
N obody gets bullied
E verybody plays nicely, like families always do
S leepovers with girls, always have fun
S o much fun with the family

Alina Choudhurry
All Saints CE (VA) Primary School , Wellingborough

Happiness Is Key

H appiness is fun
A time for friends and family
P laying out in the hot, bright sun
P atience is on the far run
I t makes people happy as a hyena
N obody is left out
E verybody is together no matter what
S leepovers go through the night
S leeping is left out so is the light.

Anika Khondkar (8)
All Saints CE (VA) Primary School , Wellingborough

Love Is Kind, Love Is Sweet

Love is kind,
Love stays in your mind,
Love is bright,
I know I'm right,
Love is light,
It represents doves,
And doves represent love.

Charlotte Pottle (10)
All Saints CE (VA) Primary School , Wellingborough

Which Emotion Am I?

I feel sweaty,
my heart's thumping,
I don't feel well,
my tummy hurts,
I wish it didn't though,
which emotion am I?
Which one,
which one?
Then something makes me smile,
I start to jump around,
I feel happy now,
I wonder why?
I wonder
what emotion am I?
Which one?

Ben Bayes (11)
All Saints CE (VA) Primary School , Wellingborough

What Is Jealousy?

Jealousy is heartbreaking,
Jealousy is strong,
Jealousy lets out a sad and sorrowful pong.
You feel as angry as a charging bull,
You feel so left out,
You feel like a pig with fire coming out of its snout.
You're feeling very loopy,
You feel like an angry Snoopy.

Emily Gamgee (7)
All Saints CE (VA) Primary School , Wellingborough

What Is Guilt?

I felt so selfish,
Because I lied to my friend,
It was guilt.

Why oh why, oh why
Did I lie to my best friend?
What do I do now?

Please, please, please help me,
This is a crucial moment,
It was deceiving...

Esabell Hemeng (10)
All Saints CE (VA) Primary School , Wellingborough

Love

Love lives deep
Inside our heart
Love makes you kind
Love makes you smart

Love makes you happy
Never alone
Love makes you jolly
And never to moan

Love can be sad
If Love goes away
So always be kind
So that Love will stay.

George Toogood (8)
All Saints CE (VA) Primary School , Wellingborough

Excited

I'm so excited,
my eyes are glowing,
my mouth is smiling,
I'm really excited!
I smile, I play loads of jokes,
my sister Katey couldn't get better,
she's the best sister ever.

Jack Cross (8)
All Saints CE (VA) Primary School , Wellingborough

Love

In your heart there is love,
it doesn't mean you push and shove.
Love is nothing that you have to find,
it never gets left behind.
Love is all you need in life,
so find yourself a husband or wife!

Manasvi Parekh (8)
All Saints CE (VA) Primary School , Wellingborough

Depression

D ark rain clouds
E ating dinner alone
P laying sad songs
R emembering happy moments
E verlasting memories
S eeing happy people pass
S itting alone in a corner
I just want to sleep all day
O n the road to suicide
N ow this is what depression feels like.

Savana Cooper (10)
All Saints CE (VA) Primary School , Wellingborough

Happy

H ow great is Happy, it comes from your heart
A small little thing cannot upset you
P lay makes me smile
P eople make me laugh
Y ou should always be happy, even when you're sad.

Izzy Clark (9)
All Saints CE (VA) Primary School , Wellingborough

Love

Love is respect
Love is a hug
Love is a smile
Never a shrug
Love is happy
Love is feeling
Love is giving
Never stealing
Love is a star
Love is a sun
Love is fire
Inside everyone.

Shabaz Rohman (10)
All Saints CE (VA) Primary School , Wellingborough

Distressed

I was distressed when I cried and
I tried to stop, but things go wrong
And I pray to have him,
Great, how do you feel when you're going to be
There? I'll pray to have him safe
So I'll remember him because he's in my soul.

Hillary-Ann Amisu
All Saints CE (VA) Primary School , Wellingborough

My Brother Jack Makes Me Happy!

My brother Jack is the best brother ever
he can't get any better
he is so nice to me when I am upset.
Jack always makes me smile
he is very good at jokes
he likes to do maths.
When he is sick I try to take care of him
he is always by my side
so I will always be by his.
When he went to hospital, I hoped he was OK
when he came home that was my day.
I am the most grateful sister in the world
I love him so much!

Katey Cross (10)
All Saints CE (VA) Primary School , Wellingborough

Untitled

Be joyful every day and this is how I explain -
When my brother went away
I couldn't keep it, no way Jose
I am happy, so is he
He is the king of bravery and he also loves me.

Grace Warboys (8)
All Saints CE (VA) Primary School , Wellingborough

Happy

I feel happy when my friends are around
and when I'm upset my friends make me smile
and if I'm alone my friends come to play
and when I'm at home I'm happy always.

Nicole Hayden (9)
All Saints CE (VA) Primary School , Wellingborough

Joy

Joy is happy
Joy is great
Joy is joy, that's all I say
Joy is amazing on my birthdays
When I'm on my roller skates
When I eat my birthday cake
Joy is joy, that's all I say.

Ellie Grace Luke (10)
All Saints CE (VA) Primary School , Wellingborough

Love Is A Feeling

Deep in your heart
you know it's true
right from the start.
Love is beautiful,
like a shooting star,
love can be close,
love can be far.

Kyle Goodwin (9)
All Saints CE (VA) Primary School , Wellingborough

Love

Love is happy
Love is kind
Love is nice and divine
Love never fails
It doesn't stray
Love wins in every way
Love is detailed
Love is great
Love is joy every day
Feeling lonely, feeling astray
Love builds it back up, every day
Just wait.

Alexander Anthony Broome (10)
All Saints CE (VA) Primary School , Wellingborough

Joyful

J ust be happy
O h, I didn't know that
Y ou be caring
F eel your mouth going into a smile
U se a brilliant smile
L ook like a nice person.

Meera Katwa (7)
All Saints CE (VA) Primary School , Wellingborough

Sadness

S adness is sombre
A ren't you glad it's gone?
D on't you know sadness has to come to a point
N ear the surface, nearer, nearer... until it
E xplodes and gives way to happiness
S o smile, don't be down
S mile, smile, smile all the way.

Aleisha Pritchard (11)
All Saints CE (VA) Primary School , Wellingborough

Joy

Joy can be anything,
Even a toy,
Joy is for everyone,
Girl or boy,
Joy should never be ignored,
Without joy you'd be so bored.

So come on people,
Don't be glum,
Sing a song, whistle or hum,
There's nothing like a song of joy,
So come on people, don't be coy.

Keira Hopkins
All Saints CE (VA) Primary School , Wellingborough

Anger!

Anger is fierce and will give people a pierce,
Anger is felt, it whacks you with a belt,
Anger is bad and you only need a tad,
Anger is hot, so don't go over the top,
Anger is a warning, so don't get mad in the morning,
Be smart and have a heart,
Because anger doesn't help,
So control yourself,
It's good for your health.

Joshua Wenje (11)
All Saints CE (VA) Primary School , Wellingborough

The Colour Of Emotions

I felt red with anger, like a tyrannosaurus rex when
it rained and I couldn't go outside to play with
my friends.
I felt worried, like a little white mouse, when my granda was sick.
I felt happy, like a hot sunny day, when I started my new school.
I felt green with jealousy, like the Incredible Hulk bursting out of his
shirt, when my brother, Evan, got a new game.
I felt blue, like the deep, dark ocean, when my granda died.
I felt red like a raspberry, when I got embarrassed singing in class.

Travis McMenamin (11)
Ardnashee School & College, Londonderry

Colour Of Emotions

I felt red-hot rage when I was hit.
I felt wobbly with worry when someone was
chasing me.
I felt jerky and jealous when I was banned from
my PlayStation.
I felt so sad when someone was making fun of me.
I felt sheepishly shy when I was kissed on the cheek.
I felt hysterically happy when I played hide-and-seek.

Dominic Hamilton (10)
Ardnashee School & College, Londonderry

My Dog

My dog wags her tail,
My dog is black and white,
My dog is cute,
My dog makes me laugh,
My dog makes me happy,
My dog likes to chase balls,
My dog likes to rest.

Tim Hirson (10)
Ashford Hill Primary School, Thatcham

Emotions

I'm Happy,
I make my owner smile, a smile that spreads from ear to ear.
When I control them, their pale face lights up
Like a light bulb and the paleness turns to rosy-red cheeks.
They feel content and cheerful, the mood that everyone likes to be in.
Sometimes I make their eyes well up and tell them to cry happy tears.
I am Happy and that's my job.

I'm Sadness,
As I take over, their body droops and their head looks down.
Bitter-sweet tears trickle down their pale face
Like the rain that trickles down the window.
Then those bittersweet tears turn to traumatic tears
And the traumatic tears turn to a weep.
I am Sadness and that's my job.

I'm Fear,
Their hands start shaking and their legs become tense.
A chill runs up their back like a group of startled spiders,
Their breath rapidly increases the longer I am in control.
I make my owner fear the worst
And to believe that something bad will happen.
I am Fear and that's my job.

I'm Excitement,
A hyper hurricane storms over them
And I can make it last as long as I want.
They feel enthusiastic about everything
And almost nothing can dampen their mood.
I sometimes make them have goosebumps
Which makes the adrenaline last longer.
I am Excitement and that's my job.

I'm Love,
Their heart flutters like a butterfly when I'm in control,
When the moment is right, I make their pale face turn rose-red,
An embarrassed smile reaches their face.
I am Love and that's my job.

Zara-Leah Williams (10)
Ashford Hill Primary School, Thatcham

Emotions

On the 19th February, I was as angry as a devil,
On the 12th March, I was as happy as a rainbow,
On the 27th May, I was as sad as a chicken,
On the 11th July, I was as unhappy as a bee,
On the 29th December, I saw emotions.

Harry Liddeatt (8)
Ashford Hill Primary School, Thatcham

Untitled

As I woke up at dawn, my dad told me that we were going to Gravity Force.
I felt like I was going to explode with excitement.
When we got there, my dad told me I would be with my half-sister,
I could not wait.
When I was on the trampoline,
I felt like a bird in flight.

Euan Fry (9)
Ashford Hill Primary School, Thatcham

That Dragon, Anger

Anger the storm cloud above your head,
Like a gladiator at a fight to the death,
You can't keep control when anger strikes you with its thunder and lightning,
When you get the urge to explode just like the sun,
When your head rolls over to a hostile
An abrupt ending with a large booming shout!

Samuel Baalham (9)
Ashford Hill Primary School, Thatcham

Happy Day

H appy, it's my birthday
A present came this way, It was a BB gun, I was as happy as a hippo
P retty clothes everywhere
P arty, party, whoo hoo, happy days
Y oung me has gone, new me is here.

Samuel Dodds (9)
Ashford Hill Primary School, Thatcham

Funny Dad

F alling off chairs
U ndoing shoelaces at unnecessary times
N ot putting up an umbrella
N ot remembering work
Y odelling in the night

D oing silly things
A lways silly
D ad keeps being silly.

Finlay Whitehouse (8)
Ashford Hill Primary School, Thatcham

The Emotion

I'm puzzled,
I'm stuck,
The water as blue as the sea,
slides as long as snakes.
Me travelling with speed,
water running fast.
Slides as steep as hills,
adventuring the scene,
being pulled underneath with fear.
Scared of which way to go,
meeting friends out and about,
having pizza after dark.

Milo McDermott (8)
Ashford Hill Primary School, Thatcham

Water Park

H appy as could be
A ninety-metre long, steep slide
P eople lining up ready for the excitement
P eople eating and drinking down below us
Y es, it's now my turn to go down, 'Wheee!'

Ted Jones (10)
Ashford Hill Primary School, Thatcham

A Day In Dubai

I woke up with as much energy as an energy drink
because I knew we were going to the beach.
Me and my family got out of the hotel
and into a taxi to the beach in Dubai.

When I got to the beach the sun was as bright as
the sand,
I wore my dad's sunglasses and ran into the sea.
After a day of fun, I went into my clean bed
to do another day of Dubai.

Dan Ward (8)
Ashford Hill Primary School, Thatcham

Aquadrome

I took one step towards the car and so did Pippa,
I felt so excited I could scream and break all the windows.
I was so silly, I was as silly as a super silly Sally
being silly,
Then I calmed down.
I was as happy as a bee, the sun hovered over
my head.
Finally, we were there; we were at Aquadrome.
Pippa's and my favourite bit was the blue slide,
After an amazing day, Pippa and I were so, so happy.

Kerry Miles (10)
Ashford Hill Primary School, Thatcham

Happiness Is Coming

My ticket's checked,
I walk into my dream,
I see it...

Happiness is coming,

The first ride is beyond my imagination,
The next one makes my imagination boring,
It is like it never ends.

Happiness is coming.

I go home,
With a happy heart,
Ready to go in the pool.

Happiness is coming.

Diving into the pool is the best part,
Swimming is the next,
Dad chased by a raccoon is something else.

Happiness has come.

Holly Campbell (8)
Ashford Hill Primary School, Thatcham

Anger Is Feared

A nger is feared
N o one has tried to face it
G oing to see the cave that is
E erie, don't
R eact to anger.

Jack Kevin McMillan (10)
Clydemuir Primary School, Clydebank

Emotions

E veryone has them
M um is stressed
O liver is happy
T im is angry
I an is shocked
O livia is lonely
N an is bored
S usan is excited

Everybody has emotions and so do I.

Rebecca Colraine (11)
Clydemuir Primary School, Clydebank

Happiness

Happiness is my greatest friend,
I am happy when you're here,
I'm happy when I eat a peanut butter and jelly sandwich.

Sometimes you come and go,
Just leaving me in tears.

But I'll see you soon Happiness,
I'll see you again soon.

Jennifer McCafferty (10)
Clydemuir Primary School, Clydebank

Emotions

E nvy is an annoying emotion because he is envious of everything,
M arvellous is a great emotion because she makes you feel good,
O ptimistic will help you feel good about life,
T ired never wants to get out of bed,
I nvisible is never seen and left out a lot,
O bsessed can't stop watching her favourite TV show,
N ice is a friendly person,
S adness isn't having a nice life and wants to be alone.

Mirren Costello (11)
Clydemuir Primary School, Clydebank

Untitled

You might be crazy or lazy,
Sad or mad, you annoy your Da and Ma,
You might be feeling happy or hoppy,
lovely or lonely in the world.
You might feel like a butterfly that is fluttering away into the sky
where it's high,
You might be a little bit scared of heights or tights.

Lucy McKibben (10)
Clydemuir Primary School, Clydebank

Happy

Happy is nice to feel,
It makes me feel full of joy,
On my horse, galloping away, I think of happy days.

As happy as a horse in a field,
Eating some grass.

I am happy when I am on my horse,
Jumping over Sadness, jumping over Sin,
Jumping over Nervousness,
Hoping he will join in.

Abbie Fox (10)
Clydemuir Primary School, Clydebank

Love Can Be All Emotions

Love can make you feel as happy as a butterfly,
flying above the grass on a hot summer's day.
But also as angry as a bull charging
at a red flag in Spain.
Love, yet again, makes you feel confused,
like when you're working out a puzzle
and you can't succeed.
But the main thing is love isn't just one emotion,
it can be all of these.

Kayla Gallacher (10)
Clydemuir Primary School, Clydebank

Worry Bag

If you see a worry bag
and your name is on the tag,
grab someone, open it,
don't get frustrated or throw a fit,
just take them out one by one,
Don't feel sad if there's a ton,
sort them out.
Might take a day,
but the worry bag will fly away.
After that you will be free
and you will always be filled with glee.
So, if you see a worry bag
and your name is on the tag,
close your eyes, count to three
and you will always be happy.

Lucy McDonald (10)
Clydemuir Primary School, Clydebank

Anger

Anger is a feeling that can change you,
so just hop into a land of fun
and be kind to everyone.
Soon Anger will run away
and leave you with a happy day.

Aimee Clark (10)
Clydemuir Primary School, Clydebank

Worried

Worry has a blue, long-sleeved top and blue trousers
with black hair.

He comes out when you think of him,
you can think of him lots of different ways
and different times of life as well.

Worry is worried when it's night,
in case some monsters are in sight,
but Worry is worried when it's bright,
because no monsters can be in the light.

Worry is inside everyone even if you're very brave,
he is always in your brain.

Morgan Grant-Cumming (10)
Clydemuir Primary School, Clydebank

Birthday Party

My birthday, my birthday comes every year,
I'm joyful when it comes and goes,
I get older by the day and older by the night,
I'm thankful when I get presents and cake.

Zaak McKenzie (10)
Clydemuir Primary School, Clydebank

My Happiest Day

My happiest day was on my birthday,
I was as happy as a sheep prancing around the field
Because my cousins were coming.
When they arrived, they went crazy as a bull charging at red.
When it came to the piñata, my cousins whacked it
Like a golf club whacking a golf ball.
When the food was ready, we stuffed our faces like pigs eating a lot of food,
When it came to the cake, my cousins sang 'Happy Birthday' to me,
They sang it like angels.
But when it came to saying goodbye,
It was the greatest goodbye I've ever had.

Benjamin Vine (10)
Clydemuir Primary School, Clydebank

Happiness

Happiness is a shining star,
It tastes like chocolate ice cream,
Happiness smells like beautiful flowers,
It looks like a shining star,
Happiness is a weapon that no one can destroy,
It sounds like children laughing,
Happiness is a friendship,
It is the best thing,
Happiness is a burning fire.

Chloe Bates
Four Dwellings Primary Academy, Birmingham

Anger

The ones we love are
the ones we hurt the most.
The bar of acceptance
is raised with passing time.
Our words,
our deeds,
evermore senseless,
hateful,
with no decipherable reason
and no rhyme.
We lash out in our increasing stress and frustration.
The ones most dear,
the recipients of our disdain.
Our anger flies in hurtful swirls,
enfolding and engulfing
and in the end, just adding
to our pain!

Aliscia Dennis
Four Dwellings Primary Academy, Birmingham

Joy

Joy
is a thing you cannot imagine
it is a beautiful thing that you feel in your heart
that makes you feel so good
that you want to shout to the whole world
you're happy with joy
and you would like to embrace all people
even those who do not know why
you're full of joy.

Mariam Assoumanou
Four Dwellings Primary Academy, Birmingham

Disgust

Disgust takes over you when something is mucky or yucky,
Disgust is popular when you see greens or peas,
Disgust tastes horrible.

D isgust
I s absolutely vile
S o are mushrooms
G arbage is disgusting
U nhappy people are seriously
S ickly
T omatoes are disgusting.

Zahra Hussain
Four Dwellings Primary Academy, Birmingham

Anger

Emerging from the darkness
like a shadow nobody wants to see.
Red and black his colour -
like a dog he barks uncontrollably.
A face as hot as fire
like a beast too furious to be curious.
Eyes amazingly intense!
Nobody likes him...
Everybody screams when he comes.
Chaos – every day growing
Light – every day failing
But Anger doesn't care!
He never did
And calming words and nice comments
While Anger is a friend.
Suddenly, light then completes his mission...
Then Anger goes away.

Hezekiah Galapon Calub (10)
Four Dwellings Primary Academy, Birmingham

Joy And Shyness

Joy has the beaming spirit of the bright, hot sun
And has the golden yellow skin that is full of happiness
and the smells of laughter and candy.
She has the sea-blue eyes and hair with the
summer dress
that reminds you of your first day on Earth.

Shyness has the memory of your first day at school
and your first friend and teacher.
Because she's the one who made you shy all the time.
She's sunset-pink, with orange hair and eyes
and has a creamy white top and has a buttercup-yellow and blue
skirt.

Ellesse Leanna Jane Reed (11)
Four Dwellings Primary Academy, Birmingham

Anger

Anger can stink like a skunk,
Anger lives where monsters and nightmares stay alive,
Anger can even be in your house, but nobody knows.

Anger burns you alive, controls you by moments,
Anger shatters your heart into chunks for eternity.

Anger is the little while when you call names and intimidate people,
Anger can go anywhere in history.

Anger can only be overcome when you say
lovely things,
Become polite for eternity,
Anger can be blown away.

George Antonio Scarlat (10)
Four Dwellings Primary Academy, Birmingham

Thrilled

Thrilled is as yellow as the sun,
Dripping lava on planets
The hot heat bursting through the walls
Thrilled is as hot as lava erupting from the sun
Blasting through the universe, creating holes
in the planets
It smells like smoke
Feeling burnt
Tastes like ash.

Farhaan Hussain
Four Dwellings Primary Academy, Birmingham

It's My Birthday Soon!

It's my birthday soon
I'm so happy, I feel over the moon,
My birthday is on Friday
and then, when that day comes,
we are going to have
cake and go whacky, sleepover and everything.
My birthday is after Easter,
I get to go
to my friend's house for a sleepover.
I get to stay for a couple of days,
so I get to play with my friend Shania
that I have known for ten years.
Now I'm so happy,
It's my birthday soon.

Kiyarnah Roya Empress Blake
Four Dwellings Primary Academy, Birmingham

Disgust

Disgust is an evil emotion, it breaks your heart,
Every day children feel this way.
People hate this emotion, it brings tears to their eyes,
The feeling of this emotion makes boys and girls cry.

Disgust is an evil emotion, it breaks your heart,
It is described in many ways,
Like repulsion and horror,
It smells like rotten eggs,
It tastes like burnt food.

Every day, children feel this way,
It all adds up in their heads
And could sometimes make them feel dead.

People hate this emotion,
It brings tears to their eyes,
It sometimes gives children the ability to cry
And also it fits in their heads like a brick wall.

The feeling of this emotion makes boys and girls cry,
Children aged one to ten can never get this emotion out of their heads again.

Eloise Mann
Four Dwellings Primary Academy, Birmingham

The Red Dragon!

Isolated, in a cave of anger,
flames burned out of his mouth,
but nobody notices the fury and rage
the beast made.
The smell builds stronger and stronger
of melting rock, but still
nobody notices.
The beast's eyes turn magma-red with irritation,
the heat was killing him
but his shield-like armour
restrained the heat from killing him,
he sat with anger in him still growing,
his scales were as red as fire.
Suddenly a noise came
piercing through his cave like thunder.
'Hello!'
The dragon's eye shot at the cave door
like a bullet; he peered with his eye
through the door, it was a child,
looking happy and full of joy.
The dragon opened the door,
the child put food on the dragon's doorstep
and ran away with a smile on her face.
The dragon's frown transformed into a smile,
his red scales disappeared and turned to
gleaming gold
and the dragon was never angry again
and stayed that way forever.

Junaid Rathore
Four Dwellings Primary Academy, Birmingham

Fear

Fear – scared of everything,
My colour is blue and purple, like stormy clouds.
Sometimes fear, sometimes it's not,
It tastes like cold food,
It smells like burnt animals,
It looks like somebody's shadow walking step by step,
It feels like being alone.

Nurain Batrisyia Roslan (11)
Four Dwellings Primary Academy, Birmingham

Anger

Anger is the fiercest emotion around,
Anger is when your face transforms to red,
Anger makes you scream, shout, punch and kick.
Anger is located in a volcano,
the volcano erupts inside you
when it is summoned.
Anger appears whenever someone calls you a name
or starts punching and kicking you.
Anger can easily destroy friendships
and any relationship you have with someone.
Anger tastes of burnt metal,
No one needs to feel anger,
because we should have a nice and kind world.
The only way to beat him
is you have to be cuddling him
and using nice words.

Joshua Evans
Four Dwellings Primary Academy, Birmingham

Anger

Anger is as red as blood
dripping from your busted knuckles
after punching a wall.
Anger is as hot as lava
from an erupting volcano.
It smells burnt,
it tastes sour.

Shania Smith
Four Dwellings Primary Academy, Birmingham

Angry Joe!

I'm Joe, I'm always angry
and stressed!
I want to go to Heaven and go back
to when I was seven
because...
then I was happy and clappy!
But now I'm angry!
No wonder the kids don't like me!
Anger just smells like cold, rotten food
and a dull, abandoned warehouse
full of loads of headless zombies.
My face is red
and I am dead!
With nothing in my head
except for...
scary old Fred!

Bradley Lewis Cheslin (11)
Four Dwellings Primary Academy, Birmingham

Sadness

My name is Cody, I'm all alone,
I was left to rot on the road.
All day I think to myself,
what should I do in life?
When I am sad, my tears are a waterfall,
my privacy is out around the world.
I am poor at night and morning,
I search for food, I beg for help.
But I hope some day, someone will help me...

Reiss Iqbal-Singh (10)
Four Dwellings Primary Academy, Birmingham

Flowers

F lowers are beautiful and smell lovely!
L ovely, different colours everywhere
O ver your garden wall are all your flowers
W ow! How beautiful they are
E very day I'm happy because of wonderful flowers
R oses are red, violets are blue, flowers are amazing
S ome flowers are so yellow, I love them so.

Naomi Fairhurst (8)
Fox Covert Primary School, Edinburgh

Scared

S uper silly zombies walking in the night
C razy, bony skeletons clashing all around
'A wake the dead, awake the dead,' all the ghosts say
'R oar!' goes the wind, all the skeletons say it will be scary all the way
'E ee!' goes the mouse, it is nearly time to go
D ash away, dash away, up into the sky. Dash away all.

Hannah Juliette Norton (8)
Fox Covert Primary School, Edinburgh

Happy

H olidays make me excited
A nyone can be happy
P laying with my friends makes me feel included
P ancakes make me smile
Y es! It's my birthday.

Rachel Hamilton (8)
Fox Covert Primary School, Edinburgh

Happy

H alleujah! It's the weekend
A cting is my favourite
P eople always make me happy!
P ocket money is wonderful!
Y um! It's apple pie!

Rosie Graham (8)
Fox Covert Primary School, Edinburgh

Dance

D ancing tap makes me happy
A mazing shoes make me dance well
N ice teachers are the best
C anada is the best place to dance in the world
E verlasting, amazing dance!

Megan Ross (8)
Fox Covert Primary School, Edinburgh

Happy

H appy is a feeling and there are lots of feelings
A tube of sweeties would make me happy
P arks full of fun would make me happy
P eas make me sad
Y ou should be happy, it's the holidays.

Murray Aitchison (8)
Fox Covert Primary School, Edinburgh

Happy

H olidays are lovely and they make me happy
A hungry tummy doesn't make me happy, but when I get food I will be happy
P resents for my birthday are so much fun
P op out of your basket you little dog, you make me happy when I stroke you
Y ou have a hamster, I hope it is happy now.

Kiana Erxleben (8)
Fox Covert Primary School, Edinburgh

Happy

H aving friends makes me happy
A ny winner is normally excited
P laying games makes you smile
P antomimes are funny and make you smile
Y ou make me laugh and you make me giggle.

Lily Teitsma (8)
Fox Covert Primary School, Edinburgh

Summer Sun

S uper sunny beaches are cool
U nravelling a blanket can begin
M unching lollies
M akes me happy
E ating ice cream makes me full of joy
R unning on the sand makes me smile

S uper sandcastles are easy to build
U nbelievable fun in the sun
N oisy beaches are fun.

Jeanie Shaw (8)
Fox Covert Primary School, Edinburgh

Furious

F luffy things don't make me furious
U p and down they run on your arm
R unning on the floor really you think I'm furious
I ncredible things make me furious
O n top of the cage the animals run
U p on the side of the cage they go
S lithering like snakes they never stop fighting.

Jacob Wilson (8)
Fox Covert Primary School, Edinburgh

Happy!

H ilarious things make me happy
A mazing, I love Xboxes
P arties make me happy
P izzas are good, but school dinner pizzas are better
Y ummy strawberries!

Katie Morrell (8)
Fox Covert Primary School, Edinburgh

Sadness

S loppy food makes me sad
A nimals sometimes sound sad
D on't make me sad
N ever be sad
E veryone will be sad at least once in their life
S ay you're a bit sad, I don't want you to be sad
S adness makes me shiver, because I like to be happy!

Devin Holligan (8)
Fox Covert Primary School, Edinburgh

Happy

H ooray, I love the holidays because you get to miss school
A n ice cream is so lovely, that is because it is so cool
P arty games are so awesome, they make me want to run as fast as a bull
P antomimes are so funny, it is never school
Y ay! It's home time! I love to play with tools.

Daniel Thomas Douglas Telfer (8)
Fox Covert Primary School, Edinburgh

Happy

H omer Simpson makes me happy because he is funny
A ctors do funny things
P ets are very funny
P izza is delicious
Y ellow custard is really nice.

Ciaran Diffley (8)
Fox Covert Primary School, Edinburgh

Angry

A rgh! Why you? You messed up my game
N oodles make me angry
G uts are weird
R oaring tigers are angry
Y ou make me angry!

Cara Watt (8)
Fox Covert Primary School, Edinburgh

Hamsters

H appy, happy, happy!
A ll the time you should be happy
M olly, oh Molly, be happy you've got a hamster
S tunning, that is stunning news
T errific, oh that is just terrific Molly!
E lie, oh no, you have too many, you'll have 14
R oyal? Will it have a cloak?
S mall hamsters are the cutest thing on Earth!

Alba Trevisan (8)
Fox Covert Primary School, Edinburgh

Angry

A rr! says the pirate
N etherlands make me angry
G us makes me angry
R ory the Racing Car gets angry when he gets hurt
Y oshi gets angry when he loses a race against Mario.

Calan Innes (8)
Fox Covert Primary School, Edinburgh

Anger

I'm the one that shows the devil side of you,
punching, kicking, it is all I like to do.
My eyes as red as blood, giving out the look
of death,
it is what I do best.
I turn your footsteps into bangs,
then I force you to kick your cabinet with a clang
When your face turns crimson, that is where the true anger begins.
Swearing and evil glaring, pushing over the bin,
Then a shriek from your mum, she cries, 'Go to your room Tim.'

Was it all worth it, do you think?
When you're going to have your punishment,
like cleaning the sink.

Archie Lee (10)
Kibworth CE Primary School, Leicester

The Angry Librarian

Creak goes the chair
and everyone turns to stare
is it the angry librarian turning to scare?
'I'll put you in the lion's room
or strap you in a chair
you naughty kid.
Why are you here to stare?
I'll pluck you like a chicken, pull out your hair.'

Zakk Batson (10)
Kibworth CE Primary School, Leicester

The Ultimate Rage!

As the anger builds up inside him, he gets more and more annoyed,
as he starts to itch with rage, he gets the urge
to attack.
He can't hold it in, it all bursts out.
the teacher sees him do it, he is now in much doubt.
He is now in the office of the creepy headmaster,
who is ringing his parents up,
he knows if he gets sent home,
his parents' punishment list will shoot right up.
His dad finds out, trouble is now about,
He now wishes he never did it,
but nobody can change the past.

Charlie York (10)
Kibworth CE Primary School, Leicester

Embarrassment

You make a noise,
You feel uncomfortable,
You're embarrassed,
Your classmates turn round,
Like googly eyes,
Staring at you.
Your face turns bright red,
Like a tomato,
You look away,
But they don't stop.
You want to look,
So you do,
But you wish you hadn't.
They're still looking at you.
They turn back around,
They stop staring,
You turn back, pale.

Ollie Parris (10)
Kibworth CE Primary School, Leicester

My Princess Of The World

Every day, you're all
I have on my mind,
My heart can't live a
second without you.

Looking at you is a
breathtaking view for all,
You are my love; nothing
will change that...

You complete me,
If anything were to happen
to you... I would live in misery;
or not live at all...
You're my princess of the
world.

Alicia Gill Fry (11)
Kibworth CE Primary School, Leicester

Nerves

Fright and fear fill my body,
An ear-piercing silence filled the deep, dark woods,
Anything could happen on this cold Halloween night,
My hands are sweaty,
Like a dripping tap,
Anyone could be looking, staring, preparing to
jump out,
I feel trapped,
I want to get out,
I cannot escape,
A tear of fear begins to roll down my rosy-red cheek.

Jess Glyn-Smith (11)
Kibworth CE Primary School, Leicester

Sadness

Sadness, Sadness, Sadness is all around
It turns the taps on in my eyes
So I have got a frown.

Sadness is in the classroom
Sadness is everywhere
Sadness is in the office
And even on my chair

Sadness is in the playground
Sadness is in the school
Sadness is in my teacher
Sadness is in the pupils

When Sadness is here
There is no cheer
When Sadness is around
Everyone has a frown.

Matthew Thomas-Emberson (11)
Kibworth CE Primary School, Leicester

Embarrassment

Googly eyes staring straight at you,
Like a lion catching its prey,
You look away but they're still there,
My face burns red like a tomato,
All those fingers pointing,
All those faces laughing.

The crowd slowly fades away,
The ground swallows me up,
Gone, gone, gone.

Amelia Eve Elliott (10)
Kibworth CE Primary School, Leicester

A Day Of Peace

Peace, peace, peace,
Yes, a day of peace,
Like kicking back calmly into a bath, with
fluffy bubbles,
Not a cloud in the blue sky,
The complete opposite of anger,
Which should be buried underground,
With no stress around,
A gust of wind blowing peace into town,
Everyone should have an aim to be calm,
Feeling calm, like a butterfly floating over a daisy,
Respect, respect, respect your time of peace,
Full of joy and hope, happiness is peace!

Libby Dodwell (11)
Kibworth CE Primary School, Leicester

Angry Game

There was a boy called Josh
Who had a game he wanted to bosh
The game made him mad
And the game was bad
So he sold it to get some dosh.

Josh Campbell (7)
Orphir Community School, Orkney

Naughty Dog Limerick

I have a sweet dog called Dolly,
She's a Jack Russell and is very jolly!
She sniffs at the ground,
And digs holes big and round,
In search of poor rabbits, oh golly!

Eva Lie (8)
Orphir Community School, Orkney

Happiness Is My Dog, Snowy

H uggable like a teddy
A dorable like a chick
P layful like a kitten
P rotective like a lion
I rreplaceable like my mum
N aughty like a baby
E xtraordinary like the universe
S nugly like fluffy pyjamas
S nowy is my dog and he is amazing.

Sinead MacLeod (8)
Orphir Community School, Orkney

The Best Party!

E veryone was excited about the
X ylophone party
'C ause it's going to be so great
I t's going to have music
T he tea is pizza
E veryone is coming
D ecided this is the best party!

Iona Garson Dundas (9)
Orphir Community School, Orkney

Free Verse – Angry, Sad And Happy!

The other day I was angry
It was like a big pool of fire
Rising higher and higher
It was like being zapped by an electric wire.

The next day I was sad
And I just could not be glad
Inside I felt really bad
I needed a cuddle from my dad.

At last I was feeling happy
And so I was not snappy
And I said, 'Let's go to Papay,'
With my little dog, Zappy.

Josie Gibbon (8)
Orphir Community School, Orkney

Anger

I felt so angry one day
And it wouldn't go away
And it couldn't stay
So after a day
I was so grey.

Gary Lee Donald Morton (7)
Orphir Community School, Orkney

Snowball Fight – Haiku

Snowball fight, don't cheat,
You put stones in your snowballs,
Ouch! That really hurt!

Keira Lowe (8)
Orphir Community School, Orkney

Excited Emotion

There once was an emotion called Excited
when he came I felt really delighted
At first he was happy
But after a while he got snappy
Then he said he wanted to be knighted.

Brooklyn Sandison (7)
Orphir Community School, Orkney

Happy Acrostic Poem

H ad a good day
A rchie liked playing games
P laying on the quad bike
P raying at church
Y es, I like football.

Archie Ballantyne (7)
Orphir Community School, Orkney

Sadness – Haiku

Sadness stops your soul
Sad stops you from standing up
Sadness sails you off.

Cody Whitton (9)
Orphir Community School, Orkney

Happy Kittens – Haiku

Got to get kittens
Mum and Dad gave a surprise
And I was happy.

Keri Ballantyne (7)
Orphir Community School, Orkney

Sad Acrostic

S he cries
A nd has tears falling
D own.

Jessica Muir (7)
Orphir Community School, Orkney

Excited Acrostic

E ach day I get out of bed,
'**X** X,' Mum kissed me when my sister was fed
'**C** ome on, let me brush the hair on your head.'
I went to school to do work with Miss A
'**T** oday,' she said, 'we are going to play.'
E veryone was excited
D oing no work made everyone delighted.

Ingrid Tait (7)
Orphir Community School, Orkney

Nervous Wreck

I have a rumble in my tummy
When I'm rolling down the hill,
I have bubbles in my tummy
When I take my pill,
Don't be lonely or you will be nervous,
I feel nervous when I'm at the doctors.

Megan Walmsley (8)
St Columb Major Academy, St Columb

Angry

A ngry is mostly what I am,
N oah, my brother, gets angry a lot more times than I do
G iant anger lurks deep inside me
R hys, one of my best friends, gets angry when I say his name
Y ou? Are you mostly angry?

Joab Stott (7)
St Columb Major Academy, St Columb

Sadness

Sadness, sadness, what a bad thing,
When you're sad have a little sing.
You will be amazed at what joy it can bring.

Everyone can be sad if you are a girl or a boy,
Remember, the smallest thing can give you joy,
Even if it is a toy.

Rhys Simmonds (7)
St Columb Major Academy, St Columb

Angry

I get angry when my friends are mean for no reason,

I get angry when I see litter left lying on the floor,

I get angry when people forget to say please and thank you,
It costs nothing!

I get angry when I see pollution on the beaches -
Animals get hurt and die!

I get angry when my neighbours don't recycle -
We have bins to do it!

I'll be happy when these things change!

Kyla Preston
St Columb Major Academy, St Columb

The Game Of Dreams

Here comes my team,
full of gleam.
Running on the grass
making a pass.
He strikes the ball
and that goal was so cool.

A substitute was made by Mr Poll,
it was me, I came on and scored a goal!
This made me happy beyond belief
and this is how I got my nickname – Chief!
The game is now almost done,
I have had a great game of football and had so much fun!

Benn Peacock (6)
St Columb Major Academy, St Columb

Friends

Sometimes I feel angry when my friends don't let
me play,
Sometimes I feel angry when they don't listen to what
I say,
I go and play with someone else when they are mean to me,
I feel like saying, 'Leave me alone and let me be.'
I curl away on my own and sometimes I begin to cry,
That's when I feel like saying, 'Goodbye!'

Emily Rose Barlow (8)
St Columb Major Academy, St Columb

The Happy Fish

I am the happy fish
my name is Snappy
I love to swim, just like Tim
It makes me happy.

Tim loves to win
I try to catch up with him
but he's already at the Trophy Cup
that's just my luck.

He always wins because he's so shiny and tiny
me and Tim are best buddies
We like to race around the lakes
our favourite food is fish flakes.

Annabelle Harris (7)
St Columb Major Academy, St Columb

My Best Goal

My favourite sport is football,
I love to watch and play,
I play with my friends at St Mawgan,
But not every day.

When I was seven, I scored a goal,
From 30 yards away,
My friends all cheered
And I was blown away.

Jacob Hurford (8)
St Columb Major Academy, St Columb

I'm Happiest When?

I'm happiest when I ride my bike
this is something I like
in the park, with my dad,
it's so sunny it makes me glad
On a Saturday, this is what we do
we also play football too.
I enjoy playing, it is lots of fun,
after all my schoolwork is done.
That reminds me to finish this story snappy,
now I can do anything that makes me happy.

Baylee Morgan (7)
St Columb Major Academy, St Columb

As I Got Angry

When I get angry, my hands get sweaty,
My head starts to turn red,
When I get angry I turn into the Hulk.
I like my friends, but not when they make me angry.
When someone hurts me and they don't say sorry, I get a bit angry.
I can get angry for lots of different reasons,
So don't annoy me,
Because I will turn into the Hulk.
I will also get revenge on you.

Alex Applewhite (8)
St Columb Major Academy, St Columb

Mountain Madness

The air that I was breathing was so clean and pure,
Carving down the mountains, I thought I would fall
for sure.
I was as fast as a cheetah chasing its prey,
My heart was beating like it was Christmas Day.
I was going down the red runs, as fast as I could,
Passing the chalets made of wood.
Swishing through the trees, spraying snow,
Spraying people because they were slow.
I was cutting through the snow like a butter knife,
Thinking, *this is probably the best day of my life!*

Evan Platt (8)
St Columb Major Academy, St Columb

When I Am Proud

Standing in front of the whole school
was cool!
I was standing on the stage and smiling my heart out.
Getting a certificate made me proud!
Everyone was clapping and cheering,
loads of smiles kept appearing.
I went back to my seat,
feeling proud from my head to my feet.
I will try to get a certificate soon,
so I will again be over the moon!

Merle Oleschkowitz (8)
St Columb Major Academy, St Columb

Holidays!

Jumping out of bed,
Jumping around like mad,
Dressed in a flash,
Dropping my suitcase, making a *crash,*
It dropped on my sister's toe,
It made her scream high and low,
Jumping in the car,
We have to go far!
Being happy and excited,
Because we are going on holiday.
And it is not tomorrow,
It is today!

Mai Oleschkowitz (8)
St Columb Major Academy, St Columb

My Anger Monster

This monster is near, it is worse than fear,
Watch out, you'll lose all doubt that Anger is here.
It makes you scream, it makes you shout,
All that energy needs to come out.

Your blood begins to boil, your heart races,
Your feet begin to do paces,
So once your shout is out,
Your anger goes away
And you feel better today.

Harriet Weller (7)
St Columb Major Academy, St Columb

I'm Excited

My tummy feels like a shaken up
bottle of lemonade fizzed up
and waiting to whoosh
and go *pop!*

Bubbles of excitement
make me want to jump
for joy
like a bouncy kangaroo.

I feel like a thousand
busy bees are buzzing in my belly
I'm excited, it's my birthday!

Lowen Battisson (7)
St Columb Major Academy, St Columb

Happiness

I feel happy when I see my dog, Dexter,
He is the best,
He makes me smile.
He wags his tail, his eyes light up,
He makes my heart feel warm inside.
He makes me laugh
When I open the kitchen drawer he knows it's full of treats,
Like bones, chews and squeaky balls
And sometimes chocolate, but don't tell Mum!
When I am feeling down or stressed
He always comes and nudges me.
He doesn't change, his love is free
and that's what makes me more happy!

George Gale-Baker (8)
St Columb Major Academy, St Columb

Happy Game

Happy hugs make us happy,
Happy days make you smile,
Playing games, I like to win.

Poppy the dog, makes me smile,
Yellow, purple and light blue flowers make me happy.

Home with my mum, playing games,
Up in my house I play games.

Great big hugs for me,
Soli the cat, makes me happy.

Maddie Watson (8)
St Columb Major Academy, St Columb

Anger

A nger is wild red
N ot happy
G reat strength grows
E xtinguishes reason
R egret comes.

Jay Cowland (7)
St Columb Major Academy, St Columb

My Birthday!

Butterflies in my tummy
Cakes that are so yummy
Friends and family in the dining room
Cats and dogs on the flume.

Violet Stevens (8)
St Columb Major Academy, St Columb

Angry

Angry is a feeling
when you are mad and sad
mixed together
You shout and scream
stamp your feet in
front of your mum and dad
Stamp your feet up the stairs
into your bedroom
and slam your door
Eventually calm down
with your mum and dad.

Joel Smith-Tallis (8)
St Columb Major Academy, St Columb

Poetry Is Not For Me!

It was snowy and cold,
A boy was walking to school
wondering about the homework and chores
He said, 'Poetry is not for me,
It makes me sad and gloomy,
I'd rather do some English
or some maths,
Because they make me smile
and laugh.
Poetry, poetry, really isn't the thing for me,
I'd rather do some PE,
or chase a bee,
Even help my mum with the Christmas tree.'
Sitting on the cold bench
saying, 'Poetry, poetry, that's not for me!'

Oliver Holloway (8)
St Columb Major Academy, St Columb

Sometimes I Feel Sad

I was as sad as a cat who's had his tail stepped on,
Sometimes I get sad when grown-ups get mad.
I had a toy plane that flew higher than the birds,
I was super sad about my precious plane,
But Mummy gave me a cuddle
Then I felt as happy as a newborn sheep.

Jessica Hubbard (7)
St Columb Major Academy, St Columb

Jamie's Poem

My dad came home from work
I ran around, I went berserk
For he had the best news
This could mean I may get a bruise!

We will have to catch a flight
Which will be at night
Where we're going is very cold
It's made of ice and snow and alpine gold.

The mountains look very high
I am so scared I could cry
Looks like we're going to have lots of fun
Bruises could appear on my bum!

We are going for a week
I'm so happy I could shriek
Dad and me are going on our own
Leaving my sister and mum all alone...

But we call them on the phone.

Jamie Lawrence Collister (8)
St Columb Major Academy, St Columb

My Cheerful Day

'A day at the Eden Project,' Mummy said,
So excited as I climbed into my cosy bed,
In my head I plan the day,
Can't wait to hear my brother play.

My brother plays in a steel band,
With his bandmates they all stand,
Watching the crowd cheer, 'Hooray!'
As the band played music today.

My cousins joined us on the ice rink,
Such a hilarious afternoon I think,
Daddy said, 'You'll keep falling over, I bet.'
I did! My bottom was soggy and wet!

Lily Isabel Dowling (8)
St Columb Major Academy, St Columb

Happy

When I am happy I feel a glow
It's deep inside my heart you know.
When I am happy my face will show
A great big smile that just won't go.
There is one thing you must know,
Being with my family gives me that glow,
They call me The Little One you know.

Lucy Honeywill (8)
St Columb Major Academy, St Columb

The Nervous Day

As hot as the sun,
Heart beating like an earthquake,
Water trickling down my hand,
Like a waterfall.
Shaking like a tree in the wind,
As scared as a mouse getting pounced on
By a cat,
As red as a red blanket,
I feel all these things
When I'm nervous.

Jasmine Rose Barley (8)
St Columb Major Academy, St Columb

Fun In The Sun

I'm happy in the sun,
I'm happy when I dance and play with my
funny friends,
In the sun I skip all day long,
I have a walk in the sun and rain, but it still
makes me happy.
When there is sun I have fun
And it makes me happy all day long,
Sun, sun, sunny sun!

Rhia Preston (7)
St Columb Major Academy, St Columb

Joyful

J umping as well as a kangaroo
O pening the door to a stunning morning
Y ummy cake on my birthday
F un at school with funny friends
U nder the umbrella on a nice rainy day
L ovely duvet day with my family.

Neve Kathleen Holyoak (8)
St Columb Major Academy, St Columb

Joyful Time

Christmas Day is my favourite time,
presents like a waterfall,
seeing half-eaten mince pies
even opening Marble Run!

It's my birthday,
I'm eight today,
I got so many fantastic toys,
books and many more.

Abigail May Hawkins (8)
St Columb Major Academy, St Columb

Being Disgusted

Disgust will make herself heard
if she sees something disgusting
or extremely absurd

She lives in a greenhouse inside your head
where she can see everything you've
smelt, touched, seen and been fed

She screams, 'Ugh and blurgh'
when you're chomping and chewing
broccoli, spinach or caviar

She'll strut out and make a hideous face
if your parents drag you
to the dreaded veg place

She'll scream and shout and make a fuss
if she sees something disgusting
on the local bus

So she'll pop out when you least expect it
if there's something super gross
that she's detected

So watch out when she disgustedly says
things like, 'Ugh, blurgh, yuck and
look at the state of the dinner trays!'

Lucy Van Yperen (10)
St Mary's CE Primary School, Horsham

Fear's A Terrible Emotion

Fear is a terrible emotion
It can be caused by a huge commotion
You'll sweat and you'll shake
And will hope you're not awake
Your stomach may start to churn
And soon you'll learn

Fear is a terrible emotion
It may give your body a notion
To run for your life
Away from all the stress and strife
But that's never a good suggestion
And you'll end up asking yourself this question -

Why is fear such a terrible emotion?

Megan Carlin (10)
St Mary's CE Primary School, Horsham

Angry World

A ggressiveness is unacceptable in the world towards other people
N o fighting, killing and no racism
G reed is the reason for poverty, ill health and starvation
R efugees are a consequence of wars
Y ell out the words, 'We have a happy world, don't make it an angry world!'

William Taylor (10)
St Mary's CE Primary School, Horsham

So, So Mad

I was streaming with anger,
it was like I was going to suffer
for my death.

My heart was pouncing
like my blood pressure
was going up too high.

It was like a beast had
shocked me for my life.

Catherine Crabb (8)
St Mary's CE Primary School, Horsham

What's It Like To Be Angry?

I was furious, my face was burning red,
My heart pulse was pounding and racing,
I was so angry, I thought I could cry and scream my head off,
I was extremely mad with anger and indignation,
I was streaming red like a powerful asteroid hurtling through space.

Joshua Crabb (10)
St Mary's CE Primary School, Horsham

Excitement

Excitement is lovely,
It makes you feel jumbly,
Inside your heart you feel love,
Floating and fluttering like a dove,
It makes you want to jump for joy,
Like at Christmas when you get a new toy,
Everyone should be happy and glad,
When they feel excited or happy, not sad,
Show your excitement by wearing a smile;
It's nice to be excited once in a while.

Amy Fisher (10)
St Mary's CE Primary School, Horsham

The Anger Poem

I was so furious,
why was it her?
I've spent hours and hours
just to see her win!
She laughed and grinned,
I just groaned,
I wanted to shout,
I wanted to scream,
I wanted to stand
and say, 'Why her?'
She smiled and smiled,
I thought calmly,
But I'm in next year!

John Newton (9)
St Mary's CE Primary School, Horsham

The Things That Make Me Happy

A friend you weren't expecting
A letter through the door
Playing in the snow
before there is no more

Manhunt, IT and football
The sunshine on your face
Birds singing in the trees
Going to your favourite place

A holiday with family
A trip out to the zoo
A hike along the seaside
and hearing, I love you!

James Gardner (10)
St Mary's CE Primary School, Horsham

The Terrain Of Terror

I had a shaky feeling
Doom waits
Sea salt boils, erupting like a volcano
Against my battered face
The sound of waves crushing one another
A monster trying to swallow me too
The Devil's cage has been opened
My worst nightmare has come true
Fear has turned towards us
The waves are at war
The pounding of my terrified heart
Is no more...

Cruz Porthouse (10)
St Peter & St Paul CE Primary School, Bexhill-on-Sea

Fear – A Standing Mystery

A barely standing statue, a standing mystery,
Draws the unknown creature into your
vilest nightmare.
Jagged claws hang from the ceiling waiting to plunge,
Screaming winds fight through the cracks
Trying to seize the dolls that guard this secret.
If somebody enters, confusion and hesitation
Would consume their innocent soul.

A howling terror terrorises the scene
A breathtaking alarm hurries down its decayed spine,
It bawls with fright like a rabbit being chased
By the fierce snake that was the family's mystery
A machine of nightmares takes over the land

The cobweb cage despises the constructive dawn
It rises from the dead
Rays of burning gold
Banishing all evil
Burning everything in its sight,
Including the ghastly house.

Alex Markham (10)
St Peter & St Paul CE Primary School, Bexhill-on-Sea

The Battle Of The Seasons

Snowflakes fall gently
Through the cold bitter air
The callous winter storm watches menacingly
The animals despair
The ground hungers
For a sunny day
Summer is so distant
It seems so far away
Pushing summer aside
The clouds cry their tears
With its murky skies, its whistling wind
Summer disappears
While the trees' jagged claws
Tears everyone's happiness apart
Winter beats summer into submission
Tearing the heat from her heart
But the battle is not lost
For the rematch will soon start...

Libby Hollidge (10)
St Peter & St Paul CE Primary School, Bexhill-on-Sea

Fear

Fear consumed my soul
Shattered windows collapsed as fear kissed my cheek
A barely-standing statue guarded by the unknown
A moaning pit of despair locked with creatures
The contraption of nightmares lifted his jagged claws
Blaring winds grabbed and drifted down my neck
As fear started to control me
Echoes amplified
Shivers flew through my spine
Thunder bellowed and rain submerged upon me
Doors creaked as the wind pushed me into the cobwebbed cage
The house sang as shards of glass scratched my head
Screams echoed from above
A sense of anxiety shoved me to the floor
The floor of wrecked arms and legs
I fell!

Lennie Peoples (10)
St Peter & St Paul CE Primary School, Bexhill-on-Sea

The Angry Ocean

The oceanic deep sea is travelling with fury
Smacking rocks with its forceful fists
With terror in its waves, the sea is full of anger
and hate
Rising like a mighty monster from the deep
And swallowing boats in one giant mouthful
The terrorising waves get fiercer and angrier
Like an avalanche of snow
Grabbing the world below
Demons of the deep
Rise from the darkness.

Joshua Jasper (10)
St Peter & St Paul CE Primary School, Bexhill-on-Sea

Winter – A Season Of Joy

The rain descends like a parachute
Jewels of sparkling diamonds
Fall to the puddled world below
Kissing the bare branches
A gentle breeze caressed the houses
A roller coaster of litter
Playing chase along the gutters
As the temperature plummets
A carpet of ice crystals
Covers the world
Winter – a season of joy.

India McCann (10)
St Peter & St Paul CE Primary School, Bexhill-on-Sea

The Happiness Of Winter

Frozen tears fall from the sky
Shining like diamonds
To a world wrapped in a warm blanket
Winter is here
As the temperature plummets
Snowflakes fall gracefully
Gently kissing the ground
Covering the floor like sherbet
Trees stand like soldiers
Tall and proud
An archway of dreams.

Jake Lister (10)
St Peter & St Paul CE Primary School, Bexhill-on-Sea

The Changing Emotions Of The Seasons

The wind took its last breath
The storm clouds cried their frozen tears
As its young melted away
Summer was coming
And the plants were beginning to smile again
Christmas was last season
Spring was coming
The sun hid in fear
Every creature was swept away
Trees screamed as frozen flakes consumed them
Winter was coming
Leaves roamed the sky like fiery phoenixes
A sea of golden wonders swept across the street
Waves engulfed the meadows
Autumn was coming
Angry fire was crackling insults at the cold
Swifts, swallows and even blackbirds soared away from their homely nest
Leaving only the strong
Winter was coming.

Gabrielle Stein (10)
St Peter & St Paul CE Primary School, Bexhill-on-Sea

The Malicious Sea

The raging storm blows through the black sea
Waves crash against the rocks as the night comes
With clouds huddled up
Boats fight against the rocks
The shrieks of people drowning
No one can continue
No one can pass the storm
The ruthless storm is as hard as rock
Nothing can defeat it
The ocean lets out the monster of the deep as it's attacked
The wind starts to howl like a wild beast
And the ocean grows stronger
As the storm is evolving
Everything starts to get tough
Like a heavy-duty soldier in war
Everyone bickers to stop the storm
But the blizzard is drowning everyone and still debating to leave
A colossal wave goes over the land and demolishes everything
Finally the warfare is over
Everything is back in peace.

Ethan Burke (10)
St Peter & St Paul CE Primary School, Bexhill-on-Sea

Taming The Angry Sea

Angry sea crashes amongst the rocks
Throwing heavy stones as if they are feathers
Waves, strong and harmful like a hurricane
Torrential rain, booming thunder and daggers
of lightning
Violent wind and screaming birds
The sea sings as it smashes against the shore
Darkness covers the world
Until dawn enters
The clouds dance away
The sea comes to a halt
And blue sky smiles over the land.

Emily Sylvia Jean Muckle (10)
St Peter & St Paul CE Primary School, Bexhill-on-Sea

The Ocean's Rage

Sailors' screams stain the air
A stairway to Heaven was unlocked
Waves swallow boats whole
As white horses run on the waves
Mother Nature slams the door
Then clouds prepare a storm
Demolishing everything in its path like a flamethrower
The ocean rages with hate
Heaven and Hell finally meet
As the ocean consumes everything in its path
Waves smear the faces of pebbles
While they howl for help
The jagged claws of the waves snatch souls away
Feasting on despair
It kills for fun!

Ella Bradley (10)
St Peter & St Paul CE Primary School, Bexhill-on-Sea

Depression – The Rundown Room

Gloomy, blacked-out place
Wakes up at midnight
Turning on the flickering light
Dusty run-down room is depressed
The thunder grumbles around the house
Like a dizzy old man
Always doing the same thing all the time
His dance never ends
Making cobwebs shiver
Sunrise to send the room to sleep.

Billy Rumble (10)
St Peter & St Paul CE Primary School, Bexhill-on-Sea

The Sea Is An Angry Dog

An angry sea is like a ravenous dog
Giant and grey
Waves like paws scratching the shore
Feeling lively and energetic
With his clashing teeth and shaggy jaws
Hour upon hour he gnaws
He bounds to his feet and snuffs and sniffs
Shaking his wet sides over the cliffs
Wrapping around me, a salty hug
Sea singing as he crashes on the shore
Skipping through the rocks
Calmed by a pure blue sky.

Ann Shaji (10)
St Peter & St Paul CE Primary School, Bexhill-on-Sea

The Changing Emotions Of The Seasons

The iridescent ice path leads to a blanket of
majestic snow
Snowmen spaced across the field
Like an army standing guard against summer -
The season of scorching heat
A slow breeze creeps slowly through the forests
Through the trees now caked in white frosting
As the wind of winter whistles intensely
The frown of winter makes some of us ecstatic and some sorrowful
Oh winter!
Summer burns through
Melting all the ice
Fish jump out to greet an immense airstream of heat
A gentle gust that volleys through the woods
A kaleidoscope of colours illuminate the landscape
The smile of summer brightens up our day
This is summer.

Connor Hall (10)
St Peter & St Paul CE Primary School, Bexhill-on-Sea

The Changing Emotions Of The Sea

The angry ocean hurls the boats
People scream as the waves soar
Whistling wind whizzing past them all
Vessels hopping up and down
Waves crushing the front decks
Sea trying its hardest to destroy them
The ocean repeatedly charges
The heavens open
Strong wind gets weaker
Aggravated ocean becomes calmer
Terrified screaming stops
Water travels down from the beach
Boats start to move
Calmness descends.

Alin Reji (10)
St Peter & St Paul CE Primary School, Bexhill-on-Sea

Anxiety – Stranded Deep

The shipwreck squawked horror
Palm trees were standing strong
Through glass shards shattering by
There was a mystical creature loitering in the shadows
Speech of the wind whined through the grains of sand
My inside was a cobwebbed cage
The land was getting irritated
Thunder hollered around me
Anxiety was rising
The terror was bundling on me
The gods of land and water were combining
To make Heaven alternate to Hell
The gust of wind drew me in
Then took me down
To never be gazed at again.

Alfie Swatton (11)
St Peter & St Paul CE Primary School, Bexhill-on-Sea

Autumnal Sorrow

The sky is grey
Full with black and angry clouds
The rain is dancing down on the crown of the trees
Like frozen tears
Gently kissing the ground
The coloured leaves are flying scared in the air
The sun is hiding behind the ugly clouds
Nature hides her green colour
Behind the autumnal oranges

The trees are standing strong
In front of the fighting wind
The clouds are still mean and black
The rain keeps falling down like silver drops
The autumn is here.

Alexia Casapu (10)
St Peter & St Paul CE Primary School, Bexhill-on-Sea

Ice Perfection

The air is frost
Cold creeps around my toes
White and dark crowds around me
Snowflakes slide off my frozen nose
Overcoats swallow me up
Mittens hug my chilly fingers
Trees stand like frozen soldiers
Ice sparkling like diamonds
Sparkling snow beneath my feet
Like a land of sherbet
Jewels of perfection fall from Heaven
Dancing through the air.

Riley Willard (10)
St Peter & St Paul CE Primary School, Bexhill-on-Sea

Fear

The turbulence inside my body is a massive wave
Like a mouth
With sharp teeth
Monster waves
Rise from the dead
The jaw of fear creeps through me
The sun has whispered her goodbyes
Darkness descends
Surrounding me in a wave of terror
Screaming ghosts of ice
Howl over my life.

Sara Maoudj (10)
St Peter & St Paul CE Primary School, Bexhill-on-Sea

Fear At Sea

The terrific claws of the sea
Rise like Satan's hand
The Devil's broken free
Once again fear arrives
The ocean is like a graveyard for boats
My desire has been destroyed
There is no hope
Sins please save me from Hell
The salt spray, like shards of glass
Attack my face
The wave is like an emerald wall
Blocking my freedom.

Ryan Graham Vincent-Smith (10)
St Peter & St Paul CE Primary School, Bexhill-on-Sea

Fear

The jaws of fear creep
Like claws of the sea approaching me
I am trapped within a battlefield
Against water and wind
Mighty waves aim their weapons
The sea is ready to eat
Waves sing to the tune of death
The sea is a graveyard
Inside me.

Sophie Western (10)
St Peter & St Paul CE Primary School, Bexhill-on-Sea

Spring Happiness

Waving in the meadow
Sunflowers held their yellow heads high
Whilst looking upon the sidewalk
The rain showers over the gloomy yellow forest
The springtime flowers peek high above all the rest
While the family of fairies rain love and kisses
And the bees whizz through green trees
For their Olympic bee race
Summer has finally come, the sunflowers cheer
as the last smell of spring waves goodbye
Flying to Heaven, the angels send messages to the
sunflowers cooking away with the sun shining down
on them.

Sydnie Pallett (10)
St Peter & St Paul CE Primary School, Bexhill-on-Sea

Terror

Claws of the ocean grab my heart
A blend of waves engulf me
Jaws of fear creep through me
Hell sent the unknown force
A killer
A powerful creature
Takes me in its arms
The Devil's cage has been uncovered.

Summer Salih (10)
St Peter & St Paul CE Primary School, Bexhill-on-Sea

The Calm Waters

The sea, the sea is where peace covers the land,
It's where the wind cleans the face of the pebbles
Squawking seagulls fly rapidly through the
snowy-white clouds,
Foaming waves dive in the calm gentle sea,
Dragon-shaped kites float high in the air
Refreshing water washes the colourful rocks,
Sails flap around the steady boats.

As the wind flows through the wooden branches,
The sun is still shining high in the clear blue sky
Pigeons soar alongside the seagulls,
And the sound of the water crashes on the rocks
Grey clouds send a warning
A storm carves the sea,
Rain drums,
The powerful wind turns the sea into a powerful beast.

Adam Barcsai (10)
St Peter & St Paul CE Primary School, Bexhill-on-Sea

The Sea's Changing Mood

Angry grey sea keeps throwing boats
Everyone screams, everyone cries
Not even trying to be calm
Wild wind whistling, always crazy
Strong waves hardly pushing pebbles
Always grey and rough
Never getting blue
Fishes sadly can't play, they're always sad
Biting the rocks
Terrible grey sea!

Calm blue sea gently holding boats
Everyone happy, everyone laughs
Gentle wind whistling, always calm
Soft waves pushing pebbles
Always blue and calm
Never getting grey
Fishes happily playing and swimming there
Sea plays with rocks
Wonderful blue sea!

Natalia Machnikowska (10)
St Peter & St Paul CE Primary School, Bexhill-on-Sea

Mystery House!

A dark building standing at the end of the road,
Tall trees crowd around,
Owls hoot as I step closer to the front door,
Fear hugs me like a blanket.
The door squeals like a mouse,
But as heavy as a brick wall,
Corner to corner, webs stick to my clothes
like Sellotape.
Cockroaches run up and down the mucky walls,
I know why nobody comes here,
Floorboards creak and moan at me,
I hear bangs and fear clings to me again!
My mind tells me, this could be the end,
Shall I carry on
And find out what the noise is, or turn back and run?
I creep up the stairs... *Bang... !*

Kelly Jenner (10)
St Peter & St Paul CE Primary School, Bexhill-on-Sea

Storm

You shout and scream at me, but I did no wrong,
You cry and make puddles, but I didn't hurt you,
You try and blow me away, but I stand strong,
I will always wait for you, but I fear you.
You break trees, legs, arms,
You drown plants to their death,
You make hurricanes in the middle of summer,
No one will ever be your friend.
Storms.

Lily-Anne Plim (10)
St Peter & St Paul CE Primary School, Bexhill-on-Sea

When The Snow Comes

No one can hear you scream,
The snow will shout louder and quieten you,
No one will rescue you,
The snow will hide you in his home,
No one will catch you when you fall,
The snow will clasp you in his own arms tight,
No one will bother saving you,
Because the snow started a rumour.

The snow will ruin you and save you just for fun,
Let you drown in sorrow,
Then pick you up just before you take your last breath,
But you can't run from the snow,
It's always ahead of you,
Chasing you before you even think about running...

Esme Forsyth (11)
St Peter & St Paul CE Primary School, Bexhill-on-Sea

A Gateway Of Light

A gateway of light,
A gaping hole in the clouds above me,
Standing in a spotlight of mystery,
Stranded in the middle of nowhere.
Fear is squeezing me so tight, I can barely breathe,
My mind not sure if this light is good or bad,
It feels warm on my cold body,
Hugging me like a blanket,
I realise this is a sign,
Fear takes over my body and grips me.

Emma Lewis (10)
St Peter & St Paul CE Primary School, Bexhill-on-Sea

The Rain Is Coming To Spoil The Fun

The waves are waving at me,
The clouds are performing for me,
The trees are dancing for me,
The people are smiling at me,
The houses are standing still, like statues,
Oh look who's coming,
It's the rain,
It's coming to spoil the fun.

And now,

The waves are jumping as high as they can, with anger,
The clouds are dark and grumpy,
The trees are fighting the wind,
The people are angry and annoyed at the rain,
The houses are dark,
The city is sloppy,
It's the rain,
It's coming to spoil the fun.

Conner Lister (11)
St Peter & St Paul CE Primary School, Bexhill-on-Sea

Wind

It brushes past my face, silent as a panther,
It taps my back, waiting for an answer,
It teams up with other elements for a play date,
Creating massacres.

It can send a shiver up your spine,
It pushes you back into place,
Just another game of chess,
Just another life to take control of.

It can lift things,
It can defy the laws of gravity and Earth,
It can punch and knock on the thickest of trees,
It can be a villain,
It can be anything it wants,
Because she is the Queen of Air,
Queen of Life,
Her name will reign in history forever.

Nothing can last forever,
Everything ends with slow or immediate death,
Except for her,
Her name means glory and destruction,
Wind.

Arran McSorley (11)
St Peter & St Paul CE Primary School, Bexhill-on-Sea

Long-Lost And Dead

Fear is a mystery that hides around every corner,
The shack sways violently as the storm grabs and shakes it,
It hides from every crack of light at dawn, just trying
to sleep,
Abandoned by the living and inherited by the dead,
Memories of children playing in the bedroom upstairs,
Before Fear took over and made the building evil,
Crumbling like a gingerbread biscuit,
Home of the dead,
Lying on the ground, weeping tears of agony,
Hell's hideout is still here.

George Fox (11)
St Peter & St Paul CE Primary School, Bexhill-on-Sea

The Light From Heaven

Hovering above the crystal waters, a bright light stood,
The Light from Heaven sat there until the moon took his place,
After that, he slept and snoozed,
While the rest of the world was in bed,
Day by day, anger built up as nobody said thanks,
Using his might, he produces lots of light for people to find their way,
Dull skies try their best to create a horrible day.
Shimmering waters lie,
Needing somebody to talk to,
Or else he will go crazy.
He will develop an emotion,
The emotion called Anger,
He will create
A tsunami!
It can happen,
It has happened,
It will happen...

Joey Burton (11)
St Peter & St Paul CE Primary School, Bexhill-on-Sea

Winter Wonderland

Crisp snow sleeping on the quiet meadow,
Little white specks plummeting,
Still, to the ground.
Icicles hanging off trees,
Freezing temperatures blast all around,
Trees lower their heads, ready to sleep,
Leaves dance joyfully to the ground,
The wind begins to howl like a wolf at the full moon,
Here comes Winter on the prowl,
Snowflakes drop from the moody sky,
Misery descends as the sun disappears,
The atmosphere, gripped by silence,
Making us shiver.

Berrie Robertson (11)
St Peter & St Paul CE Primary School, Bexhill-on-Sea

The Sea

Rough, spitting bubbles,
Explosions of white mist into the air,
Punching the golden shore,
Enormous,
A fighting machine which batters and bruises,
Grey, aqua waves meet the sky,
At the horizon the grey sea distances itself from above,
The sea of storms,
The ferocious waves raging with anger,
Time to strike back on the Earth,
Stormy god of the sea,
Hell was broken into Heaven above,
The white horses arrive to have a play date with the storm's death.

Millee-Rose Leverington (11)
St Peter & St Paul CE Primary School, Bexhill-on-Sea

The Sea's Day

Wavy, like the long locks of her hair,
As beautiful as the Queen's crown,
Crashing with anger and hatred,
Smooth as a baby's cheek,
Fighting to break free from their clasp,
Stones rolling like a game of chase,
Babbling with fun,
The salt running through each wave,
Boats struggling with fear,
Leaping like a lynx,
Grumpy like an old man,
This is the tiring day of the sea.

Emily Rose Day (10)
St Peter & St Paul CE Primary School, Bexhill-on-Sea

Winter

In the winter,
God be with me, help me,
Help me to pass through the malevolent storm,
In the unscrupulous wind,
I battle through the rough winter air,
I stand frozen in the emotionless frost,
Will I be able to escape?
You laugh at me with anger,
You know you are taking over the world with your harsh weather,
Wind breaks the arms of trees and freezes leaves on the spot,
You terrify me and hug me with fear,
Fear of the unknown,
Strong as ten thousand men going into battle
And as noisy as the bombs and guns they will use.

Raymond Nyabakari (11)
St Peter & St Paul CE Primary School, Bexhill-on-Sea

The Sea

The sea rocked back and forth,
waving as passers walked by.
Sometimes the sea feels lonely and frustrated,
crashing over boats,
sending fishermen overboard.
His mocking laugh made the waves get hurled as high as skyscrapers
and the people stay away.
When the sun peered over the horizon to say good morning,
only then, the sea became calm.
People come and walk by.
Swimmers splashing in his clear, turquoise waters,
multicoloured fish splash in the cool waters, vibrant colours mixing against the bright morning sun.
Then the sun would slowly go down.
Then the sea would feel lonely again.
All he could hear was his own breathing and the gentle rocking of his waves,
just like a lullaby,
rocking away into deep, deep sleep.

Eleanor Klein (10)
St Peter & St Paul CE Primary School, Bexhill-on-Sea

The Dismal Day

The sea was calm and relaxed,
Enjoying a peaceful afternoon nap,
The sky was miserable and depressed,
Moaning and groaning of boredom,
The day was dismal.
A burst of light pushed its way through the clouds,
Surrounded by the shadows,
Excitement erupted within the day,
Hoping it would see the sun again,
Like a door to Heaven,
Offering hope and freedom,
The light that the day wanted, had come.

Bo Louise Reed (10)
St Peter & St Paul CE Primary School, Bexhill-on-Sea

Anger Is Hate...

Anger is red,
red like fire,
it flows through the body
just like lava.

Crackling and roaring,
like a wild beast,
pawing the ground like a bull,
rearing like a wild horse.

Hatred's army came riding in,
on monsters and nightmares of darkness,
arrows red like blood rain down,
leaving joy lying dead on the ground.

The Grim Reaper comes towards you...

Grace Keenoy (10)
Sampford Peverell Primary School, Tiverton

I'm Upset...

I'm upset,
I feel caught in a net,
I've been insulted,
Called names.

Joy fighting to get free,
To get out of its cage,
Fear locked up trying to plea
And anger in a rage.

Raindrops falling,
Happiness calling,
Tears rolling down my face,
In a race.

People cracking jokes,
Is what I really need,
To get rid of this feeling,
I need to laugh

And this process has nearly begun...

Oscar Shaw (9)
Sampford Peverell Primary School, Tiverton

Sadness

A sea full of sadness,
sad times all remembered.
Ripples in the water with tears,
you can hear *tip-tap* of water,
you put on a slow tune of sadness,
it's raining heavily outside my window as far as
I can see,
sad colours surrounding me, that makes me feel sad.

Ellie Churchill (9)
Sampford Peverell Primary School, Tiverton

Anger

Anger is red,
As red as a Devil.
You are now on fire,
you think of the colours red and yellow,
The anger gets bigger and bigger,
until you let the bomb go *bang!*
Then the anger flows around!

Harry Pengelly (10)
Sampford Peverell Primary School, Tiverton

Happy

When I see something I like,
I feel as happy as a joyous bunny.
I am happy when I'm in my garden
with my family.
The flowers are as lovely as a kitten,
I like playing with my brother
as we jump over shadows.
I will be my happiest
if I owned my own boat.
I want everyone to be happy!

Coşkun Tom Basma (10)
Sampford Peverell Primary School, Tiverton

Anger

Angry, laying on his bed,
shaking his head,
wishing his friend never said,
look where it has led.
Now we're broken up,
thinking he's upset,
now's the time to reflect.

Lewie Maycock (10)
Sampford Peverell Primary School, Tiverton

Joy

Joy is when the sun is out,
when you can go to the beach and mess about,
swimming without a care,
his wife relaxing over there.
Just like a war between Joy and Anger, Happiness
and Frustration,
Joy is like a Christmas and Anger is like a
bad Halloween.

Kian Sugden (11)
Sampford Peverell Primary School, Tiverton

Joy

Joy is when the sun is out,
when you can go to the beach and mess about,
swimming without a care,
his wife relaxing over there,
like lizards in the sun.

Connor Banbury-Parkhouse (11)
Sampford Peverell Primary School, Tiverton

Joy

Joy is something that comes from your heart,
Joy is a party that goes off in your head,
Joy can be a sea full of happiness.

Joy can express what you are feeling,
Joyful is when you are really happy.

Joy is all the colours of the rainbow,
Joy is something that doesn't have negativity.

Joy makes me feel more than happy, more than excited,
Joy makes me feel the next big thing!
Joy is everything in the whole world.

Dani Clarke (10)
Sampford Peverell Primary School, Tiverton

Joy

You're going to slide down your favourite ride,
Joy keeps you happy even when you're unhappy,
Just don't be mad, just be happy.
You should be happy or joyful,
Have fun and don't let anyone dim your fun,
Go and have fun in the sun on a bouncy castle.

Shannon Kathleen Toon (10)
Sampford Peverell Primary School, Tiverton

Anger

Anger is red
Just like a fire
With orange and yellow
It is like a bomb exploding
You try not to unleash it
You try to stop
Anger is painful
Like when you fall over
Sometimes you can't control it
Not many people like it
Anger clouds you, surrounds you, it's all around you.

Joshua Aldridge (10)
Sampford Peverell Primary School, Tiverton

Oceans Of Love

Dolphins diving in a moonlit sky,
stars like diamonds in the night,
by the sea and the lapping waves,
they meet and share the magical day,
holding hands as the moon comes up,
laughing, happiness, they're falling in love,
moonlight shimmers across the sea,
aquamarine stretches to the horizon
as far as the eye can see,
gazing into each other's eyes,
dawn comes and the sun starts to rise.

Stephanie Curnow (11)
Sampford Peverell Primary School, Tiverton

Streams Of Tears

When sadness comes beware
the tears will come but will wear you down,
Sadness streams out of you like the River Thames,
don't let it put you down, if it does,
pick yourself up again,
as long as it takes, you can pick Sadness up
wherever you are,
it is like placing a stick into the river.
If you're down, don't lock yourself away,
the sun goes in, the moon comes out,
twinkling stars come out wherever you are.
You have to scream and shout and let it all out,
don't try to hide, just let it out.

Molly Tidborough (11)
Sampford Peverell Primary School, Tiverton

Happiness

Happiness is beneath, in your soul
Happiness will be all day long
Happiness is used everywhere I go
Happiness goes everywhere I know
Happiness is in love
Happiness is in your heart
Happiness is bringing people together
If your life is not happy then life is a bad dream.

Holly Partridge (9)
Sampford Peverell Primary School, Tiverton

Frustration

Frustration is like a fire burning within your soul,
It is like fireworks exploding everywhere, some spin round and round,
while others shoot right up into the sky.
Frustration feels like falling from a high building,
slowly tumbling down to the ground. Why?
It is an ocean filled with salty tears,
It feels like no one cares.
Taking a long walk in the glistening sun
can repair your thoughts.
Your body feels free at last,
No longer holding onto your past.

Matilda Clothier (10)
Sampford Peverell Primary School, Tiverton

Sadness

Sadness is a funny thing,
empty and blue,
It makes you want to be alone,
with no one around you.
Slowly your spirit walks away
and you will be lonely
the next day.

Amelia Edwards (11)
Sampford Peverell Primary School, Tiverton

Birthday Girl!

Surprise! Surprise! Today's your special day
go down to the barn and find what's munching
on the hay.
You scream, then you shout and you let it all out,
Then you cry out of happiness and run to the door,
peering through the bars you see what's on the floor.
A pony! A pony! you squeal with delight,
then you push on the door with all your might.
You cling onto Hony,
the name of your pony.
Then we sing Happy Birthday,
for you're a very lucky girl.

Teiana Tanton (10)
Sampford Peverell Primary School, Tiverton

Scary Sounds

Sudden scary sounds send shivers down Suzy's spine,
Spooky shadows and shapes surround Suzy.
Terrifying tarantulas team together, terrifically,
Snakes slither suspiciously seeking succulent food.
Dark, dingy dungeons damage life.
Bees buzz beautifully, but petrify me,
Rats really are the most disgusting things ever,
Frozen in fear forever.

Beau Jones (9)
Stoke Bishop CE Primary School, Bristol

Sadness

In the layer of your head lives Sadness.
A melancholy creature of blue.
Flying about on a rain cloud,
Inside of you.

Causing a new River Nile,
As lonely as ever,
Sadness is one of the most important emotions,
That will stay with you forever.

As silent as a soldier,
As major as the Queen,
Just think of Sadness up on her cloud,
When someone's being mean.

Gracie Joyce (9)
Stoke Bishop CE Primary School, Bristol

Anger

As I felt my feet get warm,
It definitely didn't feel the norm.

As I felt my face go red,
I badly needed to go to bed.

As I felt my heart pump fast,
You'd better watch out, it might go blast!

Hannah Woodfield (9)
Stoke Bishop CE Primary School, Bristol

Old And Longing

I'm a shadow on the sofa, waiting for you to
come home,
We were always together, now I'm alone.

I cry because I never got to say goodbye,
Your last words trick my mind, they seem to be a lie.

The dip where you used to sleep, left behind,
There's no one to tug the blankets now, I don't mind.

An empty space at the table, your favourite chair,
Why is life so unfair?

I am now in a cold, abandoned space,
When will I leave this place?

Lilly Vincent (9)
Stoke Bishop CE Primary School, Bristol

Nervous Tennis

Stepping onto the tennis court
My heart is in my mouth
All I am hoping
Is that the umpires don't call 'Out!'
A shiver runs down my spine
They are serving first
With nervous energy
I think I'm going to burst
The ball as green as can be
Hits her racquet
It comes shooting at me
My racquet is ready to strike the ball
Thwack! I hit it
My return is good, my confidence is rising
I won the point
A few minutes later
It is my turn to serve
I threw the ball high
And hit it with a clever curve
But it curves too far
My confidence drops
My nerves kick in
I throw the ball up...
Here we go again.

Olivia Daniels (10)
Stoke Bishop CE Primary School, Bristol

A Lovely Sunny Day

The sun is bright,
the sky is blue,
everything looks wonderful
as wonderful as can be.

The wind is whistling,
the trees are wrestling,
everything looks wonderful
as wonderful as can be.

The trees are collapsing,
the branches are dancing,
everything looks wonderful
as wonderful as can be.

The river is rushing,
The animals are prancing,
everything looks wonderful
as wonderful as can be.

Nature is wonderful,
as wonderful as can be,
it always puts on a show
to make everybody pleased.

Zuhayr Abdullah Ahmed (10)
Stoke Bishop CE Primary School, Bristol

Untitled

I'm nice and cheerful,
I'm the opposite of anger
And people mostly see me
When there's lots of laughter.

Everybody really likes me
And nobody dislikes me,
Unless they're not in the mood,
Or if they're very crude.

What am I?

Happy!

Martin Meilus (10)
Stoke Bishop CE Primary School, Bristol

End Of School! (Happy)

It's 3:30 and the bell rings,
The happy children grab their things,
As they charge towards the door,
And almost drop their stuff on the floor!
Chatting about the time to come,
They're sure to have lots of fun!
In the playground, pulling on coats,
And shoving chocolate down their throats.
As the sun shines in the sky,
The children feel like they can fly,
Girls and boys skip and run,
Hooray! At last school is done.

Freddie Brown (10)
Stoke Bishop CE Primary School, Bristol

Happy

H appiness puts a smile on your face.
A t a celebration happiness is everywhere.
P arty! Party! That's what makes you happy.
P eople you love make you happy.
Y ay, yay! It's your birthday!

Harry Shouls (9)
Stoke Bishop CE Primary School, Bristol

Volcano Explosion

Trapped inside, about to erupt
clouds of smoke tearing up.

Where to look, where to hide,
what's going on deep inside?

A recipe for disaster
about to strike.

Dashing rapidly high up like a cloud
the unbearable lava fills the calm sky.

Despite the bright red racing through my mind
there lives a relaxed soul.

Just then I start to realise
there is no need for anger.

As calm waves chew across the shore
the ruby lava gracefully floats away.

Alex Bennett (10)
Stoke Bishop CE Primary School, Bristol

Anger

He is as red as a tomato,
He is about to explode,
He's coming round the corner,
He's flying down the road,
All you can see are the flames dancing
on his head,
Black smoke fills the streets,
Everyone goes mad,
Anger is back,
Anger is back!

Cleo Holmes (10)
Stoke Bishop CE Primary School, Bristol

Sunday Happiness

Half awake, half aware,
In my soft, silent bed my splintered eyes stare
At a dead-wind, dull day.

Thoughts start to spin like a Ferris wheel,
This dreary day offers elation
As scrunched-up socks catch on the heel.

Speedily dressed, required gumshield in,
Excitedly focused and ready to go
Tackety boots tap, *determined to win!*

Ecstatically edgy amongst eager team players,
Doggedly dodging through sludgy, slime mud,
Happiness bursts in soaring layers.

Finley Evans (9)
Stoke Bishop CE Primary School, Bristol

Joy Forever

J oy is a ray of sunshine
O ut in the meadow wide
Y ou are prancing through the lovely grass

F lowers are smiling at you
O n you go, feeling warm inside, while
R uby-red roses stand out in the grass
E very second clouds pass overhead
V ery pleased to see you joyful once again
E verything is blissful
R abbits dance energetically through the daisies.

Annabel Denning (10)
Stoke Bishop CE Primary School, Bristol

Anger

When you have a frown
and your smile is upside down,
Well here's a rule when you're angry
try to stay cool,
It feels like the beaming sun burning on your head,
when you burst finally your face turns red.

Please don't take the anger out on other people,
try and keep it for yourself instead.

Listen to this poem, it's for health as well.
It bummers when it thunders,
sometimes just stay happy,
say no to the thunder and say hi to the sunshine,
it will dry up the rain and thunder.
It's time to chill, it's not fair for you to be angry
and make the right choice, make sure you don't take it out on
someone.
Please stay healthy, anger can affect you and make you very ill,
please, just relax and rest, stay healthy and safe.

Laila Chodkiewicz (10)
Stoke Bishop CE Primary School, Bristol

My Angry Family

My younger brother often gets angry
When he doesn't get his own way,
He screams and he shouts and he gets very cross,
When he doesn't get his favourite candy.

My dad sometimes gets cranky,
When he isn't allowed the TV,
With a shake of his head,
He goes straight to bed,
So I threaten him with a hanky.

My mum sometimes does get upset
And she cannot stand it if I make her wait,
When I ignore her basic instructions,
She only becomes more irate!

Now, the one thing that makes me angry,
Is when I want to play with my phone,
I'm quite often called, but ignore them quite frankly,
I just want to be left on my own!

Keira Taylor (10)
Stoke Bishop CE Primary School, Bristol

Happiness

H is for horses galloping in the breeze
A is for the art and the paintbrush agrees
P is for pandas sleeping in the sun
P is for playing, I think it's fun
I is for ice cream the yummy, scrummy joy
N is for nature, the thing I most enjoy
E is for eco, the thing I have to do,
S is for sunshine, the star that's never blue
S is for swimming, the sport I love to do

But all these things are better when I'm doing them with you!

Pippa Davies (9)
Stoke Bishop CE Primary School, Bristol

I'm So Mad But Really Sad

I'm so mad
but also really sad

I might be crazy
but only maybe

I'm so mad
but also really sad

I might be jealous
so please tell us

I'm so mad
but also really sad

I might be angry
but also hungry

I'm so mad
but also really sad.

Noemi Korenova (10)
Stoke Bishop CE Primary School, Bristol

Happiness In America

When my parents told me
That we were going to see
My fabulous American family,
I was as happy as a buzzy, busy bee,
Bringing back nectar for his queen.
On a jumbo jet, we flew high across the bright
blue sea.
We landed with a bump, hours later, in New York City.
Then on to Pittsburgh, where we finished our journey.
Three weeks we spent there that summer; the days were hot and
sunny.
Happiness sailed on an ocean of sweets and frothy
root beer.
And it clung like a newborn baby to his mummy,
To the fun of Great-Grandma's 90th birthday party.
Meeting aunts, uncles, cousins; going places I've
never been.
Watching a baseball game, while eating a delicious hot dog, all mean
To me, happy, jolly memories that make me so keen
For another holiday with my American family, far across the Atlantic
Sea.

Sonny Snell (9)
Stoke Bishop CE Primary School, Bristol

Happiness

I am a laugh lover,
a smile maker,
I make you feel jumpy,
even when you are grumpy.
You may even gaze,
in amaze,
I make you feel alive
and want to jive,
you won't get teary
for I am with you.

What am I?

Flo Richards (9)
Stoke Bishop CE Primary School, Bristol

Don't Be Sad

Don't be sad.
because then we'll feel bad.

Have some fun
without the sun.

Make sure you're happy,
even when you're wearing a nappy.

Don't give yourself pain
in the rain.

Gilly Thorne (10)
Stoke Bishop CE Primary School, Bristol

Storm

I always dreamed of a horse called Storm,
Tall, dark and gallops through the thorns,
With a little white mark on his furry head,
Oh how I dream of him whilst laid in bed.

Canters on through the fields, with his three
white socks,
Now we come to halt by the docks,
But until this day, I will stay sad,
I know this dream will come true and I'll be glad.

Ananya Allen (10)
Stoke Bishop CE Primary School, Bristol

Chloe's Feelings Poem

When you feel joy, your spirits come to life
When you feel sadness, you feel lonely and scared
When you feel anger, you want to rage and shout
When you feel fear, your heart beats faster and you want to run away
When you feel disgust, you think something
is disgusting
And want to get away
When you feel disliked, you feel like you don't have any friends
When you feel loved, you feel like others care for you
And you're not alone,
You're safe.

Chloe Low
Stoke Bishop CE Primary School, Bristol

Disgust

The wild, whispering wind blows past,
You're annoyed,
You don't care about anything.
You've been in the light and now you're in the night,
No one wants to be around you,
You are miserable,
The twinkling stars have vanished, it is as black as midnight.
I feel like the darkest green that has ever been,
I don't want to listen to anyone,
I hate anyone that annoys me,
My hair is swishing like mad,
I am going to break out!

Ruth Louise Hetherington (8)
Stottesdon CE Primary School, Kidderminster

Guilt

Tearing me in two,
I wish I knew,
How to stop this force beyond my control,
Repeatedly stabbing me in the heart,
Who is behind this evil art?
Guilt

It has spilt all over my life,
Since the tilt,
Which shook my life,
Ever since that fateful day,
When lies turned my way!

Charlotte Edge (10)
Stottesdon CE Primary School, Kidderminster

Anger

He's a red monster deep down inside,
When he jumps out others hide,
He's as red as a ruby, with hair like fire,
Hands on his hips, his eyebrows are as thin as wire.

Don't you dare annoy him,
Or he'll be angry to the brim,
He never thinks about what to say,
And what he does makes others feel grey.

He's an evil, little, angry man,
I am definitely not
A fan.

William Kenneth Ellison (10)
Stottesdon CE Primary School, Kidderminster

Anger

As the red mist descended
Anger filled my heart
Rivers started to flow
A monster rose from down inside
And gave me an unearthly look from my side

The firework gets lit
And it is so bright I hide in fright
And once I get started
I give it all my might

A spear hits my heart
And breaks me apart
Growing in a fiery rage
I stop, and come back to Earth again.

Tom Harris (11)
Stottesdon CE Primary School, Kidderminster

Anger

When the monster shows its face,
Nothing can be replaced,
During your anger phase,
You put them all in their place,
When the temperature starts to rise,
You're all clogged up inside,
Because you're so annoyed,
Your fuse shorted even more,
When you're asked to do something by your boss,
No one knows when you'll set off.

Tom Bore (11)
Stottesdon CE Primary School, Kidderminster

Love

Love tosses your heart around,
Tugs it in all different directions,
Trying to stop your face blushing as your heart pounds,
Your affection fills in its last section,

Every time I open my eyes it is there,
Blinking like the stars twinkling,
I realise how much I care,
Our whole life together until we start wrinkling,

I sit watching it bubbling up inside me,
That is what happens when two hearts collide,
We will never divide,
You will always be by my side,

Your hug covers my heart with love,
One day we will be together up above,
Love keeps your heart in shape,
Smothers you with a cape,
This is the power of love.

Maisie Erin Walter (11)
Stottesdon CE Primary School, Kidderminster

Jealousy

Rumbling resentment as fierce as a dragon,
Perfectly protective in every way,
But jealousy is something we have every day,
When someone is sharing you want to shout, 'Enough!'
Jealousy is an emotion which is very tough.
Jealousy is a problem we need to take to the bay,
Not hold inside to let it eat us away,
Green with envy your heart fills with doubt,
Wash it all away and get it all out.

Molly Bergman (11)
Stottesdon CE Primary School, Kidderminster

Worrying

When I worry,
I hate food like curry,
I always do,
Sometimes do you?

I worry like Mom and Dad,
Do you think that's bad?
I cry in bed,
Which hurts my head.

When I feel down,
I think of a clown,
I don't like clowns,
They advertise them in towns.

Recently I moved lands,
With my bare hands,
I moved to a town,
Oh, I might see a clown.

Why did I have to move house? Why oh why?

Lydia Baggott (9)
Stottesdon CE Primary School, Kidderminster

Anger

When I'm angry
I call Mr Happy
The red on my face
Fades away
My face turns back
To normal when my
Anger's gone away and
I've calmed down so I can
Have a happy day.

When I'm angry my face
Turns red and I get all hot and sweaty
So the only cure is to
Take deep breaths so
It all fades away and
I can have another happy day.

Joseph Michael Myerscough (9)
Stottesdon CE Primary School, Kidderminster

Anger

Descending in a fiery rage,
A power that gets stronger with age,
The blazing eyes feed on fear,
It hits you like the sharpest spear,

Living in the darkest deep,
Waiting to make the strongest weep,
As rivers of fury run through me,
Its wrath is stronger than can be,

As fires burn in my soul,
I start to lose power and control,
Intense blazes burn my heart,
It kills my joy with a single dart.

James Williamson (11)
Stottesdon CE Primary School, Kidderminster

Jealous

As the green mist rose,
A tear fell upon my nose,
Jealousy stays in my soul,
And will be there until I grow old.

When I feel jealous I get very blue,
And all I need is a hug from you,
Jealousy gives me a horrible stitch,
And makes my personality twitch and switch.

When I get jealous it makes me mad,
That is why my personality goes bad,
When I get jealous I am torn apart,
I feel like there's nothing in my heart.

Grace Jolliffe (9)
Stottesdon CE Primary School, Kidderminster

Sad And Happy

I am on an edge with joy,
Leaping in circles, circles,
A smile has appeared on my face,
The joy, the joy,
A sun has beamed in my heart like a shooting star in a night's sky,

My tears are like bullets pouring down my face,
I run, I hide, I weep,
My heart is in pieces,
They have shattered across the land,
I feel like a burnt out star.

Isla Griffiths (9)
Stottesdon CE Primary School, Kidderminster

Fear

When I'm lost,
When I'm lonely,
When I come across my enemy,
This is what I call fear.

Happiness all crushed up,
Put into one big cup,
Given to the monster under my bed,
This is what I call fear.

The spider creeping up my nerves,
The sound of gunshots,
People fighting on the streets,
This is what I call fear...

George Fierek (10)
Stottesdon CE Primary School, Kidderminster

It's Lonely

It sits outside, under the old oak tree all alone,
It stares up at the glittering stars and the bright crescent moon.
It had moved from house to house,
Then school to school!
It wasn't familiar with its surroundings,
It couldn't call its new house its home.
Tears ran down its face,
As the stars twinkled above.
Abandoned, afraid and alone it wept in the shadows,
Like a lost child.
The night crept on as it sat under the ebony night sky.

Evie Davies (10)
Stottesdon CE Primary School, Kidderminster

Regret

Why did I tell her?
Will she say it to the teacher?
Can it be fixed?
Could it affect reports?

Butterflies swarm in my tummy,
Will the school tell Mummy?
My mind's getting tight,
Would it go alright?

Doubts, nothing but doubts,
Just focus,
Is there a spell?
Hocus-pocus.

It was supposed to be a secret,
Why oh why,
Am I untidy?
Does it show?

Keep calm, keep calm,
Breathe, will it soon go away?
I have to tell,
But what to say?

I've told,
It will be ok,
My regret that took over my life,
Has finally gone away!

Evie Clinton (10)
Stottesdon CE Primary School, Kidderminster

A Happy Poem

Scoring a goal makes me as happy as can be,
Going on holiday makes me as happy as can be,
Having a smile makes me as happy as can be.
Although it takes a while, it can feel good to give someone a smile.
Jumping in a pool makes me as happy as can be.
When I'm happy, I try not to be a fool.
I feel as happy as can be when I can be me.

Daniel Horsley (10)
Stottesdon CE Primary School, Kidderminster

Anger

It lives at the bottom of a deep dark cave,
With scaly red skin and fiery hair,
An orange moustache and spiky feet,
The other emotions hide from the deep.

In his cave, under their feet,
He listens to the laughing that is torturing him,
This feisty emotion is angered to the brim.

When he hears the sound of annoyance,
Scarlet smoke rises from the cave,
A monster flies over his clenched hands,
And through his fists.

Bill Halliwell (10)
Stottesdon CE Primary School, Kidderminster

Excitement

I think... Excitement dresses green, like it can't be seen,
I think... Its socks are covered in bright pink spots,
I think... It delivers butterflies, for a good reason,
It is here and now every season,

I think... She really can't wait to visit,
I think... She knows it will be exquisite,
I think... She is everywhere, every second,
It is amazing how she is there when she is beckoned,

I think... It dances and sings for people waiting,
I think... It gives excitement to the world debating,
I think... She loves her job,
Because everyone has an exciting life.

Amber Kimberley (9)
Stottesdon CE Primary School, Kidderminster

Aaron's Anger

A fearsome beast
Spiky thorns digging in
A big, ginormous body
It's a pitch-black sky every night
Fireballs in its eyes, that's where it really hides
Burnt skin, like being put in an oven.

Aaron Cawthorn (9)
Stottesdon CE Primary School, Kidderminster

Hannah's Happy Poem

I am very happy,
But also chatty,
It's so much fun
To be happy in the sun,
I am happy at school,
With a ball,
There's a water park
With a dog's bark,
I get happy dreams,
Without any screams,
The clouds are made out of candyfloss
With a rainbow stripe across,
The air feels bright,
With a lot of light,
Now I am going to sleep,
Without a sunlight peep,
I'm waiting for the new day,
Without a delay.

Hannah Williamson (8)
Stottesdon CE Primary School, Kidderminster

Sadness

She huddles up in the playground,
She comes out when you're feeling blue,
When she's left out of games and ignored
Like a wild boar,
These are the things that make her come up,
She's the saddest girl in town
Because no one
Wants her around.

Emily Evans (9)
Stottesdon CE Primary School, Kidderminster

Quinn's Anger!

When you are angry,
You go as red as a rose,
You act like a bear,
Who's just had a mare,
You glare and you stare,
Your eyes see red,
You're mad,
And you're bad,
You hate everyone around you,
Then all that makes you better
Is hugs and nice words.

Quinn Milo Walter (9)
Stottesdon CE Primary School, Kidderminster

Dreaming

It's sometimes good, sometimes bad,
It might make me feel sad,
In it, I am lost,
I do it every day,
I can choose it, whatever I say.
My lip might twitch,
I usually lie down,
I could frown.
I would be in my Dreamland,
It might be fire in my head,
I lie, scared, in my bed.
It could be joy,
About a boy.
I might be scared about a monster.
I could be singing a song,
That is very long.
My eyes carefully closed, like mice toes.

Jasmine Edge (8)
Stottesdon CE Primary School, Kidderminster

Love

Love,
You could fly like a dove,
You could breathe like a pug,
Feeling snug in a rug, having a hug.

Love,
You rise above,
You shove yourself down below,
Breathing very slow, just give me a mo.

Love,
Flap about like a glove,
When you're pink, you can link and wink,
When you blush, you will feel lush and crush.

You are loved forever.

Bethan Price (9)
Stottesdon CE Primary School, Kidderminster

Shocked

All of sudden it comes across your face,
What is happening?
Your heart stops beating and the world stops working.
Sometimes you feel sad,
Sometimes you feel bad,
Your mouth widens,
Your eyebrows rise,
You body freezes in the breeze.

Shocked!

Grace Harris (9)
Stottesdon CE Primary School, Kidderminster

Scared

In the dark, gloomy cave,
Nobody gives me a wave.
I just sit on my own
And shiver in the cold.
You're an invisible ghost,
Not like a party host.
You feel sad
And always bad.
I shrink inside,
With nowhere to hide.

Scared!

Max Parker (9)
Stottesdon CE Primary School, Kidderminster

Happy

I am happy playing drums at home, sitting in my bedroom alone.

Please Mr Bully, tell me what I've done,
I just wanna be happy and be with my mum.

Please Mr Bully, tell me what I've done,
I've just got my sweat all around my collar.

Zakarri Royston Johnson (11)
The Linden Academy, Luton

Joyful

Xbox one makes me happy.
It has the best games ever.
Xbox one is as fantastic as a Lamborghini.
Xbox one is a box filled with achievements.
It's dark green, sparkly silver and it's white.
Xbox one is better than school.
Xbox one is also better than ICT and it's better than playing outside.
When you're about to play on it, the music is very, very, very loud.
When the music is very very loud you would feel like saying stop,
stop, stop!

Amaan Kazmi (10)
The Linden Academy, Luton

Sadness

Sadness is the worst thing,
It feels like a sharp pin.
It will sink your happiness down and deep,
When Aunty Reese was forever asleep.
The death of her made me feel weak,
The death of her meant I can't sleep.
I will never forget Aunty Reese,
She helped me with bullies so mean.
When people put pressure on me,
I always go to Aunty Reese.
Rest in peace, Aunty Reese.

Tinuke Oluyomi Otudeko (10)
The Linden Academy, Luton

Excited

Boom! goes the popper!
The poppers fly in the sky like planes.

Boom! goes the popper!
The poppers are noisy as an elephant.

Boom! goes the popper!
Having tasty food.

Boom! goes the popper!
Party games are fun.

Boom! goes the popper!
Jumping up and down.

Boom! goes the popper!
Having fun in the sun.

Boom! goes the popper!
Birthday parties are exiting.

Boom! goes the popper!
Using the piñata is delighting.
Yeah! Yeah! *Boom!*

Malaika Malik (10)
The Linden Academy, Luton

Anger

At a house, Anger is like a mouse
It slips in and out
It tells you what to do when your parents
are telling you
It might go crazy, when you are eating broccoli
Anger rules over fools who believe it
It runs away when joy is on the way
It can take a while, but when it climbs things get vile
Anger is seen every day, especially when it rains, Anger is like fire.

Christopher Zander (10)
The King's House School, Windsor

Anger, Sadness And Joy

Anger is always angry, like an angry bull,
When Anger is really angry, his head lights up, on fire.
I hope you never have Anger in your head when you go to bed.
If you wanted Anger to stop being angry,
You need Sadness to cry on Anger's head to put out the fire
And to stop Sadness crying,
You need to ask Joy to put things right.

Micah Odufuwa (7)
The King's House School, Windsor

David's Victory

The Philistines were scared off this planet
The Devil's fear had taken them prisoner
Goliath shouted all through the night for someone
to fight
Out in the pastures, David fed sheep
His courage was strong in the Lord
He gave his kin food for he had a promise to keep
He saw the giant, who said,
'Give me a fight or I won't go to bed.'
David's courage jumped up and down
He told his idea to the king
Saul gave him armour to bring
He gathered some stones in his sling
For scared he was not
His courage jumped up and down
During the fight no one was bored.

Hayden Redmond (10)
The King's House School, Windsor

Disgust

Onions smell so horrible, they smell like a
scared skunk,
My pet skunk has a bed bunk.
Stinky (my skunk) never uses his spray,
So instead he burps any way.
Stinky's burps are so smelly that they can kill one hundred elephants.
When Stinky burps in the water
It is so smelly and bubbly that you can smell it ten miles away.
Stinky is smelly and small, very small indeed,
I don't know, but Stinky is so silly that he might
have a need.

Abigail Simpson (8)
The King's House School, Windsor

Happy, Happy, Happy

I am so happy that I could scream out loud!
I am so happy I could turn round and round,
I am so glad I will never turn sad.
It is my birthday!
You see you silly lad, if I am sad I turn mad,
I like to bake a chocolate cake.

Keziah Navarro (9)
The King's House School, Windsor

The Exciting Poem

I am excited when I see my nanny,
I have an exciting family,
I have an exciting dog,
I have a head to nod.
I am excited to make a new friend.

Millie Ellis-Missin (8)
Upton Cross Primary School, Liskeard

My Dream Horse

When I see a horse,
I am amazed so much,
I want to ride them,
Once I got to ride them
I was so happy.

The horse was trained,
talented and playful
It was as gentle as
a wonderful rabbit

The amazing coat was white,
and had black spots,
It had a black mane,
which swayed in the wind

When I ride it
I feel relaxed and excited.
I wish I could keep the horse
forever.

Izzy Alleyne (7)
Upton Cross Primary School, Liskeard

My Lovely Cats

Cats make me happy,
I have three at home.
They eat stinky, squishy food,
They are sometimes angry,
Sometimes not.
My favourite cats are Willow, Tiggy and Lily,
They are cute, they love me,
I love them,
Cats are what I love.

Jessica Alders (7)
Upton Cross Primary School, Liskeard

My Dog

My dog is called Zak,
He is as brown as coffee
And he is ten.
He makes me happy because he rolls around
like a bouncy ball,
He is a bulldog and Staffy.

Nicole Kirkham (8)
Upton Cross Primary School, Liskeard

Happiness

Happy is when you're loved,
laughing,
smiling,
cheerful,
joyful.
After laughing you will smile
and keep laughing till it's out of your system.
Parties are fun,
Parties are funny when clowns fall down.
It's fun when you're happy,
Nice when you smile when it's bright at night.
Elephants don't smile, but humans are different,
Stars shine and you will too,
Stars shine brightly at night.

Aled Griffiths (10)
Ysgol Glan Cleddau, Haverfordwest

Sadness

S adness is when you're hurt, sad or crying
A fter sadness comes happiness
D oing harm to other people makes them sad
N o smiling if you are sad
E ndless sad face
S ad, sadness, sad face
S adness involves sad faces.

Lachlan Elrick (10)
Ysgol Glan Cleddau, Haverfordwest

Anger!

Anger is an emotion you feel when you are
angry, annoyed or even sad.

Some people are easy to make angry, but
some people are not.

The ones that are easy to make angry are
not angry for long.

But the ones that are not easy to make angry,
well, you'd better watch out!

Max Peter Fraser Tytler (10)
Ysgol Glan Cleddau, Haverfordwest

Despair

When something very, very sad
Happens in your life,
Something inside you changes
And you suddenly hate your life.

Your every memory suddenly seems sad
And sadness becomes despair.

It takes over,
Controls you,
You lose your will to live,
It feels like happiness has died.
When
you
feel
despair.

Efa Gardner (10)
Ysgol Glan Cleddau, Haverfordwest

Fear

My heart is pounding
Like a beating drum,
My hands are shaking
My legs are numb.

My palms are sweating
My legs feel like jelly,
My throat is dry
I've got butterflies dancing in my belly.

The day has come
I'm full of dread,
It's finally here
I wish I was safe back in my bed.

My name is called
I can't make a sound,
I open my mouth
My voice can't be found.

All eyes are on me
My time has come,
I take a step forward
It's finally done.

Ffion Lucy Roberts (10)
Ysgol Glan Cleddau, Haverfordwest

She

Her lips were smiling,
A little glint in her eyes,
Positivity and ecstasy running through her mind,
Pleased with the joy in her life.
Young and grateful to be alive.

Emily Hartley (10)
Ysgol Glan Cleddau, Haverfordwest

Despair

In a cave
Where is the light?
Why won't daybreak come?
How am I to fight?

Bolted are the doors,
That rattle with hate
And shout at my hope,
Or destroy my fate.

First it was my family,
Then gone was my breath,
Choking, suffocating, dying,
Is this depression, despair or death?

Blinded by my last golden hope,
The only colour I know is death,
So far down, where is up?
Have I had my last breath?

No head under the hat,
No foot in the footstep,
No voice left to shout,
At the darkness of the depth.

Death! No.
Unfairness? No.
Depression? No.
Despair... Yes.

Brooke Evans-Harries (11)
Ysgol Glan Cleddau, Haverfordwest

Anger

School is a bore,
I want to roar.
A furious, friendless fantasy,
Waiting for the bell,
It's time to yell.

My mind's going dark,
All because of Mark,
At this stage, I'm ready to rage.
I'm going mad,
Anger is bad!

Mia Elliott (10)
Ysgol Glan Cleddau, Haverfordwest

Jealousy

Have you ever felt jealous?
Well that's spontaneous!
Usually all your friends disappear,
But after you make amends they reappear.
At night you hear the jealous lad,
He repeats in your brain, 'You've done bad'
The playground seems so big,
You're sweating like a pig.
You hear the words, 'Best friends; you're so kind;
Listen, I have something on my mind!'
You look fierce, feel frightened,
Someone comes over to you and your day lightens.
You go over to the person you've hurt,
'Listen, I'm sorry!' you blurt.

Isabelle Watts (11)
Ysgol Glan Cleddau, Haverfordwest

Black

I held my breath
closed my eyes,
crossed my fingers,
faced the skies.

Whispered for help,
couldn't see.
Why wasn't anyone
coming for me?

I sat down softly.
I was sitting on air,
it wasn't like
a bed or chair.

I searched hard
for any sight
of living things...
Then I saw light.

I lay down in the light,
safe from harm.
Smelt it, tasted it,
this moment of calm.

This was the life,
but then came fear,
as a big black shadow
prowled ever near.

I closed my eyes.
Held my breath.
This was Black
and Black was Death.

Seren Griffiths (11)
Ysgol Glan Cleddau, Haverfordwest

What Am I?

I feel the pain,
The pain I have felt many times before,
I shed a tear
And then...
Boom!
I cry like a waterfall.

What am I?

Sadness.

Emyr Jones (11)
Ysgol Glan Cleddau, Haverfordwest

Emotions

Joy, what a wonderful word,
Warmth, delight, no sadness to be heard.
I see my laughing lamp light up with glee
And the excitement coursing up my trembling knee.

But here comes Sadness,
What a horrible stress.
My heart, it's like a fading star,
That lives under an ugly scar.

What about fear?
It's like a Viking with a spear.
Waves of feeling, change people and places,
Emotions are erratic, why change their faces?

Evan Thomas Watts (11)
Ysgol Glan Cleddau, Haverfordwest

What Feeling Am I?

My nerves are pounding out of my
hard hand,
I am sweating like a pig!
In a persistent, pouring
puddle of doubt,
I am a never-ending shower.
Fluid drenching my small hands,
I am sitting in a puddle,
Oh no, it's my go!

Tomos Gwilliam (11)
Ysgol Glan Cleddau, Haverfordwest

Hate

H atred is a speeding bullet
A nger infused with jealousy
T o punch through a wall
E vil hides inside.

Dafydd Brân Pawlett (11)
Ysgol Glan Cleddau, Haverfordwest

YoungWriters
Est.1991

Young Writers Information

We hope you have enjoyed reading this book – and that you will continue to in the coming years.

If you're a young writer who enjoys reading and creative writing, or the parent of an enthusiastic poet or story writer, do visit our website www.youngwriters.co.uk. Here you will find free competitions, workshops and games, as well as recommended reads, a poetry glossary and our blog.

If you would like to order further copies of this book, or any of our other titles, then please give us a call or visit **www.youngwriters.co.uk.**

Young Writers
Remus House
Coltsfoot Drive
Peterborough
PE2 9BF
(01733) 890066 / 898110
info@youngwriters.co.uk

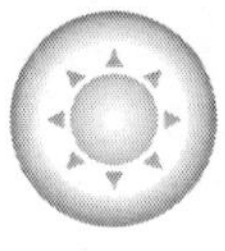